Return of the Raven

SUE COLEMAN

Art and Design by: Sue Coleman

www.suecoleman.ca

Printed by: FriesenPress

www.friesenpress.com

Distributed to the trade by The Ingram Book Company

**Dedicated to my family
with love.**

Prefix

In the beginning...

the world was covered with water. Gods lived in the sky and only creatures that could survive on, or in, the ocean inhabited the planet. Through an unfortunate accident involving a shaman of the sky, who had been digging for roots around a tree, two sky children, a brother and a sister, fell through the weakened soil. They tumbled, along with the tree, it's roots, seeds and soil, towards the water covered planet and were spotted by a swan who managed to catch the children on his back, saving them from drowning.

It was impossible to return the children to their home in the clouds, so, after much thought and discussion, the creatures of the sea brought the dirt, grasses, seeds and tree up from the bottom of the ocean. They spread the dirt on the back of the giant sea turtle and planted the tree and seeds.

The children stepped off onto the first land.

Occasionally the earth moves, that's because the giant turtle gets stiff, once in a while and needs to move his feet.

As the years passed, the children grew. The boy became a young man and was a very good hunter and provider. He loved his sister dearly and was very protective of her.

His sister however gradually became extremely unhappy. As she got older, she began to feel that something was missing in her life, although she didn't know what it could possibly be. The older she became, the more she began to seriously contemplate ending her life. She considered the many ways to die, but all seemed too painful.

One day she was sitting by a stream, thinking her unhappy thoughts, when she spotted a beautiful, egg-shaped stone lying in a pool. The thought crossed her mind that if she swallowed this stone it would surely *kill her.*

Without giving herself a chance to be afraid, she picked up the stone and swallowed it. Miraculously she didn't die, instead, the stone grew and many months later she delivered a beautiful baby boy. She called him Raven.

Knowing her brother would be jealous of her baby, she took Raven to her friend, the heron, to be raised. Years passed and when Raven reached maturity, the heron returned the boy to his mother.

As expected the brother was extremely jealous, and he immediately began plotting a way to kill Raven. He decided to take him on a hunting expedition, and on the very first day tried to fell a tree on top of Raven. But his young nephew had been born of stone and the tree broke as it came down across his back.

After several misfired arrows, badly set traps and rock slides had failed to kill Raven, his enraged uncle turned to the ocean, demanding that it rise up and drown his nephew.

The waters rose up, flooding the land, but Raven, having been raised by a bird, put on a coat of feathers the heron had given him as a young child and flew up into the sky.

The land had been completely covered with water for many moons and Raven was tired of flying. Spotting the top of a mountain sticking out of the water, he came in to rest on the peak. Tired and exhausted, he fell into a deep sleep.

When he woke, he realized the water was finally receding and many more of the mountains were exposed. He was hungry and as there was nothing to eat on the mountaintops, he decided to fly out over the water in search of a meal. He soon spotted a newly exposed, sandy, spit of land that was covered in shellfish, crabs and delicacies of every shape and kind. Circling, he came in to land and, hopping along the beach, he ate and ate, until he could eat no more.

Now he was bored.

Looking around for something to play with, he thought he heard some squeaky little voices coming from somewhere. Curious, he began flipping over rocks and shells looking for the source.

About half way up the beach, he came upon a giant clamshell and flipped it open. The inside was full of tiny little people, all struggling to escape. They had black hair and dark brown eyes just like Raven, but whereas he had a coat of feathers, they were completely naked.

He was so full of seafood, he decided not to eat them and instead he would teach them how to live on the new land. He would help them find food and clothing.

He would no longer be bored

Sue Coleman

as he was sure they would be very entertaining.

These people were the first Haida from the lands of the Haida Gwai.

Trouble with Raven

Year 2000 and something.

Raven circled. The clouds hung heavy over the bay and the seagulls were clustered along the shoreline. A few were half-heartedly pecking at the bits and pieces washed up in the tide line. The rest were huddled together each trying to find protection as the wind ruffled their feathers.

As usual the raven was hungry,

although of late his appetite had been waning, things didn't taste as good as he remembered. He drifted down to settle on an old stump that was half submerged in the sandy silt of the delta. The tide was going out and he could feel the spray being carried by the wind as it lifted the tops of the waves and threw them at the beach. A lone heron was feeding in the tidal pools.

'Tough old bird,' thought Raven, but then, you had to be tough these days or damned patient. Food was scarce although the heron didn't seem to mind, patience was his philosophy, the food would eventually come to him. It always did.

Raven watched as the heron plucked another morsel from the water. He ruffled his feathers.

"Must be some of the old spirit," he grumbled to himself.

Every time he tried to use his spiritual powers it backfired on him. His father and all the fathers before him, way back to the beginning of time, had trouble with the spirit. There was no way of foreseeing the outcome, the spirit seemed to have a mind of it's own. Still, it would be handy about now, if only to whip up a decent meal.

Moodily he turned his back on the heron and looked across the tidal flats to the shore. Tucked in amongst the trees at the foot of the mountain were

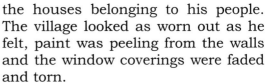

the houses belonging to his people. The village looked as worn out as he felt, paint was peeling from the walls and the window coverings were faded and torn.

Scattered around the houses was an interesting array of modern technology and shopping carts. Raven frequently stopped by to check things over, always on the look out for new additions to his collection.

Sparklies were his favourite, pieces of shiny metal that reflected the sun and himself. Most of the sparklies were too big for him to lift, which was a shame, because after a while they didn't sparkle any more.

They died.

The rain killed them.

Raven was very protective of the pieces he had managed to save from the brown-rusting rain disease. He had carried them to a secret cave, half way up the side of the mountain. There he had carefully arranged them so they could catch what light there was coming in through the narrow entrance. It made the cave come alive, even on a dull rainy day.

It made him feel close to ...

Close to what?

Well, he really couldn't say but he felt close anyway.

There, he didn't feel alone. Maybe it was all those reflections of a very handsome bird, a bird that was always willing to listen.

Sue Coleman

Up there, in that cave, he could talk to himself, or at least to his reflections, without feeling stupid. Sometimes it was almost as if they talked back.

Other birds would have said he was crazy if they knew.

Maybe he was.

Looking back again at the ramshackle collection of houses he spotted a new addition to the pile behind the end house. It looked promising, but this morning he didn't feel in the mood to go prospecting. It could wait a few days. One thing was for sure; it wouldn't run away.

He had no idea why his people discarded their treasures, leaving them outside to rot and rust. Especially the ones shaped like boxes that roared and raced around on wheels. He knew that the people rode inside them and when the box stopped roaring, the people got out. Sometimes when the roaring died the people would open it's mouth and poke around inside until it started roaring again.

Well he would roar too if someone poked around inside his mouth.

But it seemed as if the spirit eventually died in everything, because there they were, along with everything else, left lying in a discarded heap, without even a decent burial.

He sighed.

'His people', they were as lost as he was. The kids playing in the yard

were as likely to pitch a stone at him if he were to visit these days.

In the last few months he had been wondering if his Great Grandfather had made a mistake those many years ago, when, in the beginning, he had taken the people under his wing and taught them everything he knew. Back then his ancestor had been honoured and respected. The spirit was wild and the world was young. All things were possible and his ancestor had been one with the spirit. He'd had his ups and downs but nothing like today.

Everything had changed when the strangers came; strangers with white skin and light hair; strangers with eyes that reflected the sky instead of the mother earth.

Were they some mad joke of his elusive relative, the White Raven? He hadn't seen tail nor feather of him in years.

But if so, how come they had no knowledge of the spirit? Instead they had brought a silent, walking, death. His people had become confused, torn apart and, now, they too seemed to have lost touch with the spirit.

He let his eyes drift past the little group of houses, up through the trees, to the cliff face. The clouds were collecting along the top of the ridge, at any moment they would open up and the rain would wash down the valley. The delta was not a good place to be. Looking back towards the trees he stirred himself and took flight heading into a tall stand of cedar.

Cedar, the tree of life, but how easily the mighty were fallen. His Grandfather had told him of times when cedar trees covered the whole valley. His people had nurtured them, only taking what was needed. Bark for weaving, roots for baskets and hats, and only the very oldest and largest for canoes and building houses. They hadn't cut down every living tree leaving the mountainsides bare and the soil eroding.

Depressed, that's how he felt. Was there nothing left that made him feel good? Depressed and hungry, where on earth was he going to find a decent meal on a day like today?

Rather clumsily, he came in to land in the branches of the largest cedar. At the base of the tree a tired old grandfather raccoon was sifting through the compost looking for grubs. He heard the ruffle of feathers as Raven settled on the branch above his head. He hesitated for a few moments listening to the muffled curses, and then, spotting a particularly juicy morsel, continued rooting through the soil.

"Morning Raven," he mumbled without looking up.

Raven perked up a bit.

"How did you know it was me?" he said. "Did the spirit tell you?"

The old coon snorted.

"Na 'twern't hard," he said, "few birds dumb enough to be out flyin' in this weather. Don't need no fool spirit to tell me who's crashing through the trees this time of the morning. 'Side's," he added, almost as an after-thought, "you dropped a feather."

"Oh," said Raven as he slumped back onto his perch. He sighed, then, with as much charm as he could muster inquired. "What's for breakfast?"

"Go find yer own," snapped the old coon, "I ain't sharin'"

Raven's eyes glinted. He looked down at the old coon.

"You wouldn't have spoken to my ancestors like that," he snapped in return. "How'd you know I won't transform you or sumthin'?"

The old coon chortled to himself.

"Bird," he said, finally looking up, "you got it real bad. Don't tell me you still believe in all that gibberish. Been sitting on the top of too many totem poles lately I see."

Raven's eyes were reduced to slits. It just so happened he rather fancied himself sitting on top of the old poles: especially the ones that depicted his Great Grandfather. Although it seemed there were all too few of them these days, and, what ones there were, too many of them had eagles at the top.

"Damned bird," muttered Raven, "always was the favourite."

Sue Coleman

Why?

That's what he'd like to know. It's not as if it was the eagle that saved the people when they were stuck in that clam shell, back there on the beach after the great flood.

And where was he when they needed fire?

Who was it that released the daylight from the box that the seagull had hidden away? It certainly wasn't the eagle.

'All veneer', he thought, 'looks seem to count for more than character. If it weren't for his ancestor taking the people under his wing, where would they be today? In the stomach of some seagull or otter no doubt.'

The old coon was still watching him.

"You need a job," he said, "too much time to think and brood. You need to work, get your mind off all that spirit nonsense. What's done is done, the past is the past, and you can't go back. Do something useful for a change. Forget it and, while you're about it, go find another tree".

With that he turned his back on the raven and determinedly went about his meal.

Raven sat for a while glaring at the old coon. He felt a stirring within him. The coon's words had hit a nerve. 'Do something useful' he'd said.

'Yeah, like what? Well, finding breakfast would be useful, but that's not what the silly old coot meant. Still, you can't do much of any use on an empty stomach.'

Raven shook his feathers, stretched and, as graceful as any damned eagle, took flight. He thought about swooping low over the coon, maybe even use him for target practice, but then decided it wasn't worth the effort. Besides, in this wind, he'd probably miss.

He caught an up-draft and glided through the great timbers, his hunger beginning to cause a dull ache in his stomach. He swung back towards the village.

'With any luck the wind will have tipped over the garbage cans,' he thought.

The first house was boarded up, some kids had sprayed crude signs all over the walls in red paint. The grass had grown up all round the house and it almost covered the abandoned car in the driveway.

The next house had dogs.

Raven didn't like dogs much, an offspring of the wolf maybe, but that's where the likeness stopped. These dogs had no pride and the call of the wild had been bred out of them. They served man, which meant that they would not tolerate Raven.

He kept on flying.

At the end of the village was a narrow dirt track leading to the garbage dump. Raven climbed a little higher, clearing the trees that surrounded the site.

'Typical of the white strangers to use the land of his people as a place to dump their discarded leftovers.' He thought. 'Not that his people seemed to care, their regard for the land was now so low, it seemed that they didn't care about anything anymore.'

Raven just couldn't understand any of it. He didn't try. If the people weren't worried, why should he be, especially as it was usually a good place to find a meal.

He circled the piles of refuse and wood slash one of the local mills had dumped, in an attempt to bury the mess, and spotted a couple of black bears. They were curled up sleeping and beside them was the rotting carcass of a deer.

Drifting down and landing far enough away so as not to disturb the bears, the raven hopped up to the remains and tore off a large juicy chunk of rotting flesh. He swallowed it whole and after a few more chunks had followed the first, began to feel much better. Maybe life wasn't all that bad. Cheerfully he hopped around the carcass, finding one meaty morsel after another. Soon he was feeling quite his normal self and, as the wind increased in strength, Raven found himself almost in the lap of the larger of the two bears. His scent was being carried away and the bear was completely oblivious to his presence.

It was too tempting; a bit of the old crafty look crept into Raven's eyes as he weighed up his chances.

"Don't even think about it."

Raven swung around. Without his realizing it, a third bear had been curled up out of sight under an old stump.

It was a small female.

"You really don't want to mess with Pa when he's sleeping," she said.

'No fun at all,' thought Raven, just when he had begun to feel the spirit rise in him, it was squashed back down again as flat as any butterfly: another of Great Grandfathers tricks.

The butterfly had been to a feast and on his way home had met the hungry raven, who rolled a log over the fat butterfly forcing him to empty his stomach. The butterfly can now only drink liquids and will never be fat again.

Raven's mind raced through the different options that presented themselves.

He could just leave, but that might make him look like a coward. He was still trying to decide whether to challenge the bear when she interrupted his thoughts again.

"Haven't you got anything better to do than irritate other people?" she asked. "I allowed you to fill yourself

Sue Coleman

on our claim. I didn't stop you, even though we were here first, and how were you about to thank us? I saw that look in your eye. Go get a life, do something useful for a change."

Raven backed slowly away, his beak hung open in shock. 'Do something useful', twice in one morning, it was all too much.

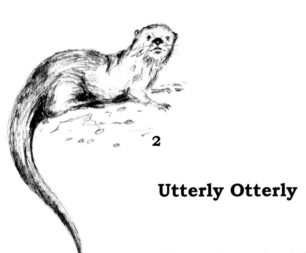

2

Utterly Otterly

Back down the hill, a river otter slid down the bank into a small creek. Just like the Raven he hadn't been feeling well lately, and the weather this morning didn't improve his mood. Normally he was a fairly easygoing fellow always ready for a romp and game of slide, but things had been slowly changing and the neighbourhood wasn't the same any more.

He had been thinking more and more of moving the family, but that had proven a little harder than he had expected. For the last few weeks he had been exploring all the tributaries that emptied into the bay. It was a very large expanse of water and there were more creeks than he could count. He was shocked to find that many other families had also had the same idea and had long gone.

Where? He didn't know.

Yesterday he had traveled through the rapids as far as the next bay, and the bay after that, but things didn't seem any better. The food was scarce and much of the shoreline had been cleared. Large houses had been built along the banks, most of which had dogs.

How he hated dogs. They ran in packs. Packs of trouble: dogs that didn't have to worry where their next meal was coming from: dogs that had a nice warm home to go to at night. Packs of pampered, over-fed and bored dogs with one purpose; to torment others. He was sick of being chased by them.

Then there were those fancy houses. A year or so ago, he had decided to check out one of them after he had spotted a hole in the foundation wall, close to the water. When he slipped inside he found the space under the house was dark and dry. He had brought his wife to see it and she had been very excited. It was the best home they had ever found. The ceiling was covered in a fluffy pink stuff that made excellent bedding and his wife had immediately set about making a nest.

His happiness hadn't lasted more than a week. Arriving home one evening after a successful fishing trip, he found the hole had been covered with a wire mesh. His frantic wife was still inside. She had heard the people banging on the walls, but was so terrified she had remained hidden in a dark corner. All night he had worked on the mesh and by early morning had managed to tear open a hole large enough for her to squeeze through. His claws were broken and bleeding from the wire, added to which, his fear of people and their dogs had festered into outright hatred; especially when his wife miscarried just days later.

At least here at the mouth of the river, because of the marches, the houses were set back from the water's edge. What few houses there were, were old, some of them abandoned. There were a lot of places to raise a family but food was the problem. Their last set of kits had not survived. They had been born weak and with problems breathing. The youngsters had only lived a few days and yesterday morning he had woken to find his mate had left too.

Now he was alone.

Sue Coleman

The otter swam down the creek and out into the deeper waters of the bay. He headed across to the opposite shoreline, there he dove, and in the mud along the base of a small outcrop of rocks he spotted a large bullhead. He had always been very lucky finding bullheads at this spot, although he much preferred a nice juicy salmon or even a rock cod. Bullheads were slippery things but easy to catch. He swam to the surface and settled down on the rocks. He tossed his head several times crunching down on the bullhead with his sharp teeth till it gave up the struggle and he managed to swallow it. He turned and dove again searching in the mud for another, it took several minutes before he had a second bullhead in his teeth and swam to the surface.

Where had all the other fish gone?

Bottom fish always seemed to be the menu of the day. Bullheads were small and it took so many to satisfy his appetite. One salmon is all it would take to have fed himself and his whole family. At one time the river used to have lots of steelhead, a delicious type of freshwater salmon, but now they were few and far between.

As he dove for the third time he spotted a crab. Tricky things, crab, but well worth the effort. He swam quickly and grabbed the crab's shell from behind. The crab's front claws were snapping in vain as the otter broke the surface of the water. He swam leisurely back to his creek and lopped up onto the bank.

Eating crab required timing and was a skill he had learned from his father. He dropped the crab, and, before it could recover, he tore off one of the front claws. The crab frantically scrambled with his back legs and, by pure chance, managed to clamp his remaining claw around the otter's tender nose.

The otter's back leg came up and, with an effort, he hooked his claws into the crab's shell and with a vicious jerk, yanked it off. The crab was flung across the bank to land upside down on a large flat rock. He lay stunned and, before he could recover, the otter had removed its remaining claw.

With the crab now rendered defenceless, the otter settled down to enjoy his meal although some of the pleasure was dampened by the agonizing sting in his muzzle.

'I must be getting old,' he thought as his teeth cracked through the shell and he tore out the juicy meat.

Raven hadn't hung around the dump. With his mind in turmoil he had fled the company of the bears, his appetite now satisfied, he decided to look for some shelter from the impending storm, and contemplate what it all meant.

As he crested the top of the trees, heading back towards the beach, he felt the first drops of rain hit his back. There was an old wharf and a creek just below him and at the end of the jetty was an old boat shed. He very quickly decided that it was the most likely place for him to find a dry perch. Apart from a few swallows there would be nobody there to annoy him and he might just get in a little nap.

The otter felt the sting of the first few drops of rain. Normally the rain didn't bother him; in fact the rain was a great opportunity to enjoy a game of slide because the banks were so wet and slippery. But the wind was rising and he certainly didn't feel in the mood for games. So, with his crab only half eaten, the otter looked around for some place to finish his meal in comfort and spotted the old docks.

Grabbing the remains of his crab he sank back into the water and swam along the shore between the pilings. He turned, following the barnacle covered timbers until he came to the rocky beach under the old boathouse.

The floor of the old house had long since rotted away and the otter could see right up to the beams that supported the roof. There was enough roof and siding left to provide some shelter from the wind and the otter settled himself down in a dark corner.

"I don't suppose you'd consider

sharing?"

The voice came from above.

"There's a couple of legs I left out on the beach, if you want them," he replied, "but you'll have to go get them yourself, I'm busy."

The raven thought about the offer, he really wasn't that hungry, but the crab did look tasty. He listened to the rain pounding on the metal roof and decided it wasn't worth the effort. Maybe the otter would get careless and he could steal a few scraps. He flew down and settled just out of the otter's reach and waited.

"You're hopeful," said the otter, swallowing a large chunk of meat. He was well aware of Raven's tricks and kept a wary eye on him.

"Oh I'm not really hungry," said Raven, offhandedly. "I just had a good meal with the bears at the dump."

The otter flicked his tail in disbelief.

"How generous of them," he replied sarcastically. "A regular potlatch was it?"

In the past a potlatch was a time of feasting and sharing of wealth. In the past there was more wealth to share.

The raven chose to ignore the comment, if he acted indifferent it was more likely that the otter would believe him and relax a little.

"How's the family?" he asked casually, trying desperately to remember when he had last seen the otter's mate. The otter stopped chewing and looked hard at Raven.

"Gone," he said abruptly, "and I don't want to discuss it over my lunch, it will ruin my appetite."

It crossed Raven's mind that such a tactic might get him a taste of that crab after all, but the look on the otter's face, kept him silent.

"Food is getting scarce in the bay," he commented, hoping to change the subject.

The otter pretended to ignore Raven; meticulously picking bits of meat that had fallen to the ground. After a while it became pretty obvious that the Raven was not about to leave.

"You could change things you know" he grumbled, "I don't know why you don't. Your ancestors wouldn't have put up with it."

Raven scowled.

"Not you as well! Always my Great Grandfather did this or Grandfather did that," he said. "I'm tired of hearing about what they did and didn't do. They didn't have things that easy, not from what I hear."

"Yeah, but at least they tried."

Raven's eyes flew open and his feathers rose on the back of his neck.

"What DO you mean?" he said, anger starting to creep into his voice.

"Oh don't get your feathers in a twist. You don't scare me. You know what I mean."

Raven's eyes took on a sulky, menacing look.

"You don't understand," he said, "if the legends are true then the spirits will do as they please; with or without my help. Whenever Grandfather tried to do things it always backfired on him. Waste of time I say, just have to learn to live with things the way they are."

Now it was the otter's turn to get angry.

"It only backfired when he was greedy," he snarled. "Greed never does anybody any good and your grandfather was VERY greedy. Always trying to steal things for himself. His powers all went to his head. Your Great Grandfather did lots of great things, then your whole family got downright greedy. But you, you're worse. You've got powers. You know you have. You're just too lazy to use them."

"Enough," screeched Raven "you think I haven't tried using my powers. You think I like being hungry all the time. I've tried, damn it, I've tried to bring salmon to the river. I've tried changing bullheads into a nice juicy trout. I've even tried transforming the rocks into flounder, but nothing works. Nothing, I tell you, nothing."

The otter shook his head, his anger turning to resignation.

"Now you sound just like the rest

---

of your family, greedy. Only thinking of yourself and your stomach. Look around you. Open your eyes. See what's happening to everything your Great Grandfather created. The world's changing, it's dying, for squid's sake, and all you can do is worry about where your next meal is coming from."

"So what am I supposed to do?" cried Raven in frustration. "You'd think it was all my fault the way you talk. People don't listen anymore."

"And why's that?" sneered the otter. "Your ancestor was honoured by the people, they painted him on their houses, carved him in wood and sang songs about him."

"Things change," snapped Raven.

"So," said the otter, "change them back."

"Damn you," screeched Raven again, "it's not that easy. The people have changed; they've learnt new things, built fast machines and have even learnt to fly. In Grandfather's time the people lived in small villages, now they live in great big noisy cities with many, many people from all over the world. Nowadays people listen to people, people don't listen to birds."

The otter gave him another of his long hard looks.

"Then be a man," he said quietly, "or have you forgotten how? When did you last transform yourself? That grandfather of yours did it all the time."

Raven fidgeted uncomfortably on the log. He was afraid it would come to this. He wasn't about to admit to the otter that he had never transformed himself. It wasn't that he didn't know how, he was sure he could. It was just that ... well; he couldn't explain it, not even to himself. If the otter knew how he felt he would call him a coward, along with everything else.

"Transformations are a thing of the past," he said, trying his best to sound superior. "The spirits worked with my ancestors to guide the people when they were young and had no knowledge of their own. I haven't heard the spirits for a long time. I think they've gone. When the white strangers came with stories of their gods, the people turned away from their beliefs and maybe the spirits died. Without their help, transformations are out of the question."

The otter looked at the raven in stunned disbelief.

"Have you any idea how stupid you sound? If the spirits were dead, you and I wouldn't be having this conversation. The spirits are life. You're alive. I'm alive. The spirits are all around us. You just don't know how to recognize them anymore; you're too absorbed in yourself. You need to go speak to Great Eagle, he'll set you straight."

Great Eagle, his Great Grandfather's old partner. Great Eagle, the generous one.

Just because the eagle seeded the river with salmon, just because he fed people who were starving, he was given all the glory. It was Eagle's feathers that were used in all the best ceremonies; nobody wanted his.

Well, if you think about it, maybe that wasn't a bad thing, but it irked the raven just the same.

"He's probably dead by now," muttered Raven, "nobody's seen him in years."

"No I don't think he's dead yet, but, it's true, he's not around here anymore. It's rumoured he went north to live, where the mountains and the sea meet, several days flight from here."

For the first time since the beginning of this conversation, Raven looked the otter square in the eyes. The only time that Great Eagle had ever really helped his Great Grandfather was in the very beginning. Then they seemed to have gone separate ways. In his opinion the eagle wasn't very smart; he gave things away all the time.

"What makes you think he would be willing to help me?" he said, as he stared at the otter without even blinking his eyes. "Eagle and Grandfather had different opinions on things even back then. What makes you think he would be any different now?"

"I told you, your family got greedy. Tell him about the people; tell him about the salmon. They say he was the one that put them in the rivers, so he's got to listen. If there is anyone that will know what can be done, he will."

"That's if he's not gone senile," muttered Raven.

The otter looked back with just as steady a stare. His pupils dilated and very, very quietly he said, "There's only one way to find out."

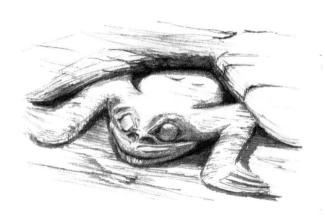

Sue Coleman

3.

Leaf-frog

The storm blew itself out during the night. Raven had flown back up into the rafters to get away from otter's taunting arguments. He'd slept badly and was not in a good mood as he flew out across the bay, soared over the cliffs that marked the entrance to a stretch of the waterway called 'The Narrows', and circled down towards his favourite old cedar tree on the opposite island. His one thought was to put as much distance between himself and the otter as possible. No matter how hard he tried to ignore it, otter's words continued repeating themselves in his head.

Towards the north end of the island was a semi-tidal lagoon, fed by a small underground spring. At the edge of it was the large twisted dead snag of cedar. How much longer it would retain its grip on the bank was anybody's guess. One half of the tree leaned out over the lagoon, the other side of the tree reached out over the ocean. Thanks to rich rot resisting oils, it's bare branches were still as strong as the day the tree had died.

Raven chose a branch about halfway down on the ocean side. Today was not the day to sit at the top where he could taunt the other birds. He needed to think and in the comfort of the old cedar he settled down to put his thoughts together.

For the first time ever his mind did not turn to food. He looked down at the waters flowing beneath him. They should be teeming with fish, instead they looked murky and left an unpleasant stain along the shoreline. The growth on the exposed rocks looked dead, and from what Raven could see through the cloudy water it wasn't much better further out. The weeds should be a rich green or brown, not dirty yellow and black. No growth, no food, no fish.

He was sure that it was better in the outer islands but here close to the river mouth and the home of the salmon, things were not good. It was almost as if it had been burned by a fire. But a fire that could burn underwater?

Raven puzzled on that one for some time before shaking his head at the impossibility.

He knew all about fire, it was one of Grandfather's first gifts to mankind. True it was the owl who took the twig and flew up into the mountains to get the fire, but it was his ancestor who planned it all and organized the animals into covering a tree with pitch. It was his ancestor that knew where the fire was kept. But, as usual, someone else got all the credit. The owl had ended up being the hero. If his ancestor hadn't seen how exhausted the owl was after collecting the fire, and hadn't flown up and dragged her back down to the tree, people would still be eating raw fish. It was unfortunate that he had shoved her whole face into the tree, but then the twig had almost burnt out, hadn't it? Besides, some people actually thought her flattened face and stubby little beak was attractive.

He sighed as he studied the river again. Yes, this was a different kind of fire although it was hardly a gift. It was invisible from above but maybe.....

Raven's curiosity was now peeked.

He hopped down a few branches then flew down to the ground. He worked his way round the tree till he reached the lagoon, all the while his eyes searching the undergrowth. Sure enough, there sleeping on a large clump of old dead moss and almost hidden by a rocky overhang was a large muddy brown frog.

Raven was not the most patient of birds but he needed a favour of the frog and to wake him from his nap probably wouldn't help him achieve his goal. So he settled down to wait, starring hard at the frog, willing him to move.

Time passed, Raven was getting more and more uncomfortable and began to get restless. There weren't any logs close at hand to perch on and the rocks were cold and damp. He looked longingly back up his tree.

"Why couldn't you be a tree frog?" he muttered resentfully.

"I hearddt thaddt."

Raven's eyes shot back to the frog, but it hadn't moved a muscle.

"You awake?" he asked.

"Who waddnts ta know?" The voice seemed to reverberate from the very depth of the frog, but still his eyes remained firmly shut.

Raven thought about the question for a moment before replying. His family hadn't always been too kind to frogs, although their kind had helped Great Grandfather in the past.

Sue Coleman

"It's Raven," he replied. "Your people helped my ancestors in the past and I was wondering if you would be so kind as to assist me in a little research."

The muscles in the frog's eyelids twitched, but still they didn't open.

"Waddt kinddt of researdtch?"

"I'd like to take a trip under the waves to check out the home of the salmon. One of your relatives took my Great Grandfather once and I'd like to make the same journey to see if everything is all right."

The frog's eyes slowly opened, with deliberation, he studied the Raven.

"This is a joke, right?" he said finally. "You cadnnt be serious. This is some kinda trick."

Raven looked taken back, the trouble with having the reputation of being a trickster, no one took you seriously.

"I'm serious," he said, "but I need a guide. It's kinda important."

The frog was amused. It had been many years since a raven had come to a frog for guidance. He was a fairly easygoing creature and quite content with his lot in life. Almost too content really, life was getting rather boring; a little adventure might be just the thing to liven things up. He had nothing to lose and it had been quite some time since he had visited the river, preferring his quiet little backwater. All the same it didn't pay to be too eager.

"Whaddt's init for me?" he croaked.

The Raven snapped his beak in exasperation.

"I'm not doing this for my own pleasure you know. I think something is wrong up the river and I need to check it out."

The frog took a deep breath and let it out slowly.

"I guess I coulddtt be persuadeddtt," he said. "But just this once, don'tttt make a habidt of it. You wanda go now?"

Raven hesitated for a fraction of a second.

"Why not?" he said. "The sooner the better."

With unexpected agility the old frog leapt onto Raven's back and, before his common sense could step in and reason with him, Raven took flight, skimming out over the lagoon and across to the mouth of the river. He looked down, assessing the depth of the water, clamped his beak shut and, without a second thought, dove into the swirling current as graceful as any diver.

Once under the waves Raven was instantly aware of how warm the water was. He was surprised; the waters in these parts were notoriously cold, varying only a few degrees between summer and winter. This summer hadn't been particularly hot, in fact

Sue Coleman

it had rained quite a bit, so what had caused the change?

They surfaced and the Raven took a big gulp of air.

"How long has the water been this warm?" he asked the frog who was now kicking strongly with his hind legs, propelling them both up river. The frog shrugged his shoulders.

"Coulddnnt say," he croaked, "been a while since I swam the river. I think it's an improvemenddnnt. Never diddtt like it coldddtt."

'Well,' thought Raven as again they dove down through the swirling waters, 'that's the FIRST thing the salmon are not going to like. I wonder if the invisible fire warms the water the same as a land fire warms the air?'

More questions and no answers, the raven pondered the problems as they swam past the tidal flats and mud banks covered with bulrush and reeds. Large flocks of Canada Geese were working their way along the bank, trimming back the grasses. The geese were long distance travelers and were getting ready for their annual flight south. Pity they were so hard to understand, they would have been a great source for information if only they didn't garble their sentences.

With the geese behind them the pair rounded a bend in the river and traveled under a new bridge built for those infernal noise machines. There were a few children playing along the bank but by keeping to the deeper waters and coming up for air under a fallen log, they swam past without anybody noticing them.

The water seemed to be changing and Raven noticed that there was a lot of strange weed floating on the surface; in some places it was so thick it seemed to choke the river.

"Preddtty lean pickin's for this time of year," commented the frog.

Raven, not used to being under the water, noticed for the first time the lack of bugs, crawfish and other river life. What was around didn't seem too lively and there was no sign of any fish at all. They rounded another bend and swam under a few more fallen trees, heading towards the old mill site, but by now the frog was beginning to tire.

"Must be getting older than I thougddtt," croaked the frog, "all this exercise, I donddtt feel so gooddtt."

Raven began scanning the banks for a place to rest, he was beginning to feel a little strange himself, when suddenly he gestured towards the far bank.

"What's that?" he said, pointing out a large concrete culvert sticking out of the opposite shoreline. The frog turned to swim towards it for a closer look but was, by now, almost exhausted. The flow of the river was too fast and, before they could avoid it, they found themselves caught in a current that had a strong acidic taste. Until now, apart from the floating weed and bits of river debris, the water had been fairly clear, now it seemed as if they were in a foggy haze and Raven had the distinct feeling that he was seeing double.

"Surface quickly," he croaked.

But no matter how hard the frog kicked his back legs, it seemed to take an eternity before they reached the surface and Raven's lungs were close to bursting. He took a huge gulp of air and then another as the oxygen slowly fed his brain and the black spots that had been floating before his eyes receded. Looking around him he spotted the frog who was looking quite ill as he floated on the top of the water.

They drifted for a short way whilst Raven waited for his travel companion to recuperate. By the looks of the frog, Raven figured there would be no going back to check out that pipe. He felt a strange euphoria, he knew he had been fortunate, although he needed to occasionally surface for air, the oil in his protective coat of feathers, allowed him to travel under water. Of course without webbed feet he couldn't travel very far which is why he had needed the frog, with his strong swimming abilities, to act as guide and mode of transport.

The frog on the other hand had not only swallowed some of the

strange looking water but his form of breathing meant he had absorbed it in through his delicate skin. Like all the other life along the riverbank, the frog was now very sick.

Raven dragged the frog over to a half sunken log and pulled him out of the water, hoping the warmth of the wood would help.

"You going to be all right?" he asked, his voice full of concern. He looked closer at the frog, whose skin seemed more mottled than he remembered.

"Get me homb," croaked the frog, "gedt me bachhhk to mby ponddtt," and with that the frog collapsed.

Raven nudged the frog with his beak, then as gently as possible he picked him up in one of his claws and took to the skies, back upstream, over the bridges where the children were still playing by the water, over the estuary, across the bay to land on the shores of the little lagoon.

He placed the frog gently on his lump of moss and wondered what to do next. He hadn't meant for this to happen. The frog looked almost dead and, by now, great sores had opened up on his back. It looked as if his skin was peeling away like an overripe plum. The pain must be excruciating. He could still feel a tingling in his own feathers, although that might be from shock.

What could he do?

If he just left the frog like this the owl, or some other creature, would most surely have him for supper.

Raven looked around and spotted a large maple leaf floating along near the edge of the bank. Fall was just around the corner and soon there would be hundreds of maple leaves covering the ground. This one was bright yellow with rusty orange tips to each of the points of the leaf. Hopping over to it he hooked it out of the water, it was still soft and supple as well as cool from being half submerged.

Raven carried it back to the patch of moss and very carefully wrapped the leaf around the frog. He stretched two of the leaf points over the frogs back legs, two over the front, with the center point of the leaf reaching over frogs head and down to the end of his nose.

The leaf clung and shaped itself to the frog.

The frog and the leaf became one.

Frog opened his eyes and took a deep breath.

"Thaddtt was close," he said, stretching his back legs one after the other, then spluttering in surprise as he looked closely at his front legs, they were a bright yellow and his feet were a rusty orange. He spun around glaring at the raven.

"Whattdd diddtt you do to me?" he demanded.

Raven was as surprised as the frog at the outcome of his actions, but was quick to recover.

"Saved your life, that's what," he snapped.

"Buttdd I'm yellow," gasped the frog. "How will I hiddtte in the muddtt if I'm this colour. I might as well have a light on top of my headdtt. Waddt am I saying? I am a light. I'll never be safe again."

"Don't you understand, you were almost dead, I didn't have much choice, there weren't any other leaves big enough. Besides, now that you look like a leaf, you can float in the water without having to hide in the mud. I think it's a perfect disguise."

Frog scowled up at Raven, hopped over to the water's edge and looked down at his reflection.

"I do look a bit like a leaf don't I?" he said as he twisted this way and that trying to see his back, no easy feat for a frog.

Raven was, by now, quite pleased with himself. Once he got over the initial shock of seeing his maple leaf hop across to the water's edge, he came to realize he had just performed his first transformation.

He'd actually done it.

He didn't know how but he didn't care, the fact was he'd actually done it.   Yes, he was very pleased. He plumped up his feathers and strutted across the beach to stand at the water's edge beside the frog.

"Not bad for a first attempt, eh?"

The frog was slowly coming to grips with the possibilities of his new disguise, but was not about to give in.

"One with a biddtt more green in it would have blenddedd beddtter," he grumbled. "This must be the briddttest yellow I've ever seen."

Raven chuckled and slapped the frog on the back with his wing.

"I think it's a great improvement over that mud colour that you were. Besides," he added cheerfully, "it'll probably wear off in a month or two."

The frog continued staring hard at his reflection.

"Don't count on it," he muttered. "Anything your Great Grandfather tranddsformbed stayed thaddtt way for good. I reckon I'm going to have to live with it. But don't you EVER combe asking for favours again. Gooddttness knows what you'll turn me into next. Bugger off up your tree and leave me alone. I needdtt a gooddtt sleep. Maybe when I wake up this will all turn out to have been a baddtt dream."

Raven hopped cheerfully around the frog.

"Your welcome," he replied with a hint of sarcasm and took off up to the very top of his tree.

For the first time in quite a while he felt on top of the world.

4

What next?

The frog was right about one thing; the trip up the river had been very tiring. It was now late afternoon and, even though the Raven found himself wanting to doze off, the familiar pangs of hunger made him decide to go back to the dump and see if there was anything left on the deer carcass. He was in luck, not only had the bears departed, there was enough scraps of meat left on the bones to satisfy the raven's hunger.

Whilst he ate he played and replayed the events of the morning's adventure in his head and, although he had the reputation for being a very smart bird, no matter how hard he tried he could not come up with any answers to his questions.

What was wrong with the river water?

How had he managed to change the frog?

When he tried changing things in the past they had never worked, so why now?

Had he done something that changed things?

If so, what?

Had the spirits returned?

Why now?

His questions just went round in circles. Round and round inside his head.

Why, why now?

His natural curiosity was seriously aroused and his success at saving the frog only added to the confusion. He began to wonder if he really could do all those things that his ancestors had done after all. The image that kept coming back in his mind was that of the foggy haze that had been in the water as they had neared that last bend in the river.

Had it come from that pipe or somewhere else nearby? More questions. Whatever it was, it had certainly almost killed the frog. It was

---

all very unsettling.

If only he understood how that transformation thing had worked maybe he could change other things after all. He would be as great as his Grandfather and all the Ravens in the past, people would look up to him and respect him again.

He spotted the old 'coon crossing the gravel road heading towards the latest piles of garbage in search of his own supper. Raven flapped his way leisurely across the road landing on the top of a rusty old car door.

"Want to know what I did today?" he asked in a casual, conversational manner.

"No," was the blunt reply.

Raven ignored it, unable to resist a little bragging.

"I turned a frog into a maple-leaf, well actually a maple-leaf into a frog,"

The 'coon snorted in disgust.

"Well that was really useful, I must say. Hopping maple-leaves, just what we all need."

"Well, you should be impressed. I saved a frog's life and transformed him. If it wasn't for me, he would be dead."

"Somehow I doubt the frog was impressed, so why should I be. 'Sides it's my guess the frog wouldn't have needed saving if you hadn't been around."

"What's that supposed to mean?"

"Go figure. You're a flying disaster,

Sue Coleman

you are. If you can't find trouble, you make it."

Raven was quite put out. The 'coon was an irritable grumpy character, which made him a great target for teasing so he hadn't expected any praise but, all the same, not complete rejection of his new found abilities. Surprise? Maybe, or even curiosity, not indifference.

"But I did a transformation'" squawked Raven sullenly. "No-one has performed one in years."

"Look around you. Do you see a line-up of frogs waiting to be transformed? Go wave your flag somewhere else. We all have our problems and currently you're one of mine. So take off and leave me alone."

With that he tore into a black garbage bag with his sharp claws, spilling the contents all over the ground in front of him. Paper plates, cups, colourful balloons and the plastic tools used during many types of human feeding practices. Sure signs that there would be leftover food. He turned his back on the raven and began to systematically sort through what looked to be the remains of a fairly large feast.

Raven was extremely annoyed and the sight of such a windfall in the paws of the mean old 'coon didn't help. If this was all the recognition he could expect from doing a good deed then what was the point?

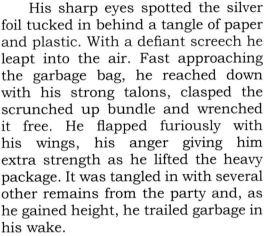

His sharp eyes spotted the silver foil tucked in behind a tangle of paper and plastic. With a defiant screech he leapt into the air. Fast approaching the garbage bag, he reached down with his strong talons, clasped the scrunched up bundle and wrenched it free. He flapped furiously with his wings, his anger giving him extra strength as he lifted the heavy package. It was tangled in with several other remains from the party and, as he gained height, he trailed garbage in his wake.

The raccoon lashed out as he saw his prize take flight, but was too late. With a cackle of triumph, Raven flew across the dump slowly gaining enough height to clear the surrounding trees. Once clear he allowed the weight of his parcel to pull him down, circling, to land on the end of the old wharf.

Napkins, streamers from burst balloons and plastic rings from the pop cans were all tangled up with the foil. It took quite a bit of work sorting it all out. Bits and pieces scattered across the dock as Raven tore away, one strip at a time.

Finally he reached the center and his efforts were rewarded when he uncovered the bony remains of a barbecued salmon. He was beside himself with glee, greedily wolfing down skin and bone, paying little attention to the accumulating flock of seagulls that had been attracted to his windfall.

Raven was used to the screeching of gulls and chose to ignore their cries, even when they started swooping down on the pieces of garbage he had discarded. One of the gulls carried off a napkin that was stained with something red. He was immediately attacked by several others; resulting in the napkin dropping to the beach where it was quickly torn to shreds and devoured.

'Fools,' Raven thought to himself as he gulped down a particularly tasty morsel. His talons firmly clasped around the edible remains to the meal, he turned his back on their taunts. From the corner of his eye he watched as one gull after another removed the other pieces of garbage scattered across the dock, including the rings of plastic.

He finished off the last of the salmon and meticulously wiped his beak on a loose plank.

'Don't you wish,' he thought as he looked up at the flock still circling above his head, waiting for him to finish, hoping he would have overlooked some scraps.

"Yach," he screeched up at them as he carefully pushed the remains of the foil between the broken planking of the dock. Laughing at their frantic attempts to reach them as they fell between the pilings, he launched himself from the wharf, flying through their midst.

'That'll keep them occupied for a while,' he chuckled to himself as he climbed higher in the sky.

The gulls, it seemed, were screaming even louder, and when Raven looked back he was surprised to find them circling around, not the remains of his meal, but one of their own; an immature gull that was struggling with something out on the mud flats.

'What on earth are those damned fools up to now?'

He flew lower, his curiosity getting the better of him. He turned and circled back gliding just above the flock. It looked as if several gulls were attacking the youngster.

Now Raven really had no love for seagulls, but this was just plain stupid. With a loud cry he swooped in to land in their midst and saw immediately what the problem was. The young gull had managed to get his head stuck in one of the plastic rings he had grabbed from off the dock. In his struggle he had tangled himself up so much he was having problems flying.

'Kids,' thought the Raven, 'can't keep their beaks out of trouble.'

"You know," he said without much sympathy, "you deserve that. You were trying to steal my meal."

He conveniently forgot the fact that he stole it in the first place.

"I think you should wear that ring around your neck for a while, it might teach you a lesson."

The young gull looked pathetic, his eyes turned imploringly at Raven just as the plastic ring ... melted.

Well it didn't exactly melt; it sort of blended with the rest of the gull's feathers. The immature gull now had a ring of pure white feathers around his neck. The plastic was nowhere in sight.

There was complete silence for all of 10 seconds as the realization that Raven had transformed the plastic and saved the youngster, set in.

The most stunned was Raven himself, he'd done it again.

How?

Was it something he said?

Twice in one day.

By the beak, he really was a transformer....

Well it wasn't quite as permanent as the frog. At least the rest of the gull would turn white when he matured. Still...

The closest of the gulls were gaping at him, their beaks hanging wide open in amazement, their eyes just about popping out of their heads. Raven, honestly, had never thought seagulls could look any dumber than they already did, obviously he had been wrong.

The birds circling above his head had started relaying the turn of events across the flats and gulls were materializing from all directions.

'Time to get out of here,' he thought, as he leapt into the air.

With a very confused state of mind, he made a hasty retreat, across the tidal flats and up one of the side creeks, looking for a comfortable spot to recuperate and rest for the night.

He flew over several pilings sticking out of the mud where, in the past, the local mill had secured their log booms. They were getting pretty rotten now but still provided great perches to sit and check out the local action. However, not this evening.

Vaguely remembering an old boat hidden somewhere in the reeds, he flew up another of the side channels that wove through the marshes. The shoreline was covered with Canadian geese, even more had arrived since this morning, a sure sign that summer was almost over.

It wasn't long before he spotted the dilapidated boat and circled down to land on the point of the bow.

Not much more than a small sailing dingy, the little craft would never float again. A few flakes of white paint still clung stubbornly to the sides of the hull but the bottom was long gone, the planking replaced by reeds and swamp grass. In the very center of the boat a small clump of bulrush had forced up a poker like seed head in mimicry of a mast. The wind, hating anything that got in it's way, had torn the top to shreds, providing great nesting material for the local redwing blackbirds.

Raven walked around the gunnel and settled down behind the reeds, on the transom of the boat. He was so very tired. Now that he was away from it all, some of the confusion faded and he began to feel rather pleased with himself. With his stomach rumbling happily, from the luxury of not one, but two evening meals, he fell into a deep sleep.

It was fairly late the next morning when he opened his bleary eyes to find his view was blocked by a large blue heron.

"Good morning. I trust you slept well?"

Always the perfect host, the heron flipped a couple of herring to Raven's end of the boat.

"Breakfast?"

Barely awake, Raven looked at the herring in surprise. He wasn't used to receiving gifts first thing in the morning and almost forgot his manners as he gulped down the herring, half expecting them to vanish.

"Th...gg..Thanks," he managed to mutter between mouthfuls.

"You're welcome; I don't often have visitors in my home. You must have been very tired; you didn't even turn a feather when I came in last night. You were dead to the world."

"Nice home," said the Raven politely as he eyed up the rest of the fish in the bow of the boat.

"Glad you like it."

The heron flipped another couple of fish in the direction of the raven before swallowing the rest himself. He was used to Raven's ways, he had watched him for a long time. There was one legend that Raven had probably forgotten, but it was a very important part of his own family history. His early ancestor had been foster parent to the Raven's own Great, Great Grandfather. It was a time before the great flood, a time when the world was young. The story was one that was told to all young heron that showed any signs of impatience as the thought of raising a young raven, with all its mischievous ways, brought on a feeling of awe and respect. It had been a difficult task, one requiring tolerance as well as patience.

"Staying long?"

Raven, not wanting to outstay his welcome, shook his beak. Maybe it was the unexpected breakfast or the patient look in the herons eye's but, suddenly, the raven found himself relating the adventures of the previous day, although he decided to leave out the visit to the dump and his confrontation with the 'coon.

The heron was the perfect

audience, being the self-appointed river keeper, he was well aware of the steady decline in the quality of life in the system. He nodded solemnly at Raven's observations on the state of the river and showed avid interest at his findings as he had traveled upstream. The actions taken by the Raven regarding the maple leaf brought a twinkle to his eyes.

Raven was so encouraged by the heron's attitude, a far cry from that of the old coon, he found himself voicing his doubts on his ability to control the transformations. He repeated all the questions that had been going through his head, hoping the heron might have some answers.

With a knowing look the heron said simply, "You'd better go speak to Great Eagle."

"That's exactly what the otter said, but I need to find him first."

"Have you spoken to the geese? They've just returned from their summer grounds in the north, they would know where to find him."

Every fall the geese had always arrived in the bay as far back as Raven could remember. They came in great flocks, mindlessly following their leader, covering the marshes as well as the fields of the neighbouring farms. Night and day they were always honking. Next to the seagulls they must be the noisiest of birds.

'An intelligent goose,' he thought,

'what a joke.'

Heron's politeness must have rubbed off on Raven, he didn't snort in disgust at the suggestion of a sensible conversation with a goose.

"I'm afraid their language is beyond my understanding, I never could make any sense out of all that honking."

"Have you tried talking to the leader?" asked the heron. "Quite a linguist you'll find, and by far the most intelligent of the flock. Watch when they come in to land, you'll want the one out front. Now I really must get back to my post, if you don't need to fly off just yet, there's fresh rainwater in that bucket by the back seat, just in case you need to freshen up. Take your time and good luck with your quest."

The heron opened his wings, stretched his long neck and with a nod of his head took flight.

"Thanks again," called the Raven. "If I hear of anything new I'll let you know."

He hopped down and took a long drink from the bucket. A quest! Was he really on a quest? It sounded quite important, almost as if there might be a purpose to his journey. He hadn't intended to blab all his problems out to the heron, but at least they had been taken seriously.

Hold on a minute, who said anything about a journey?

Well there wasn't much he could do around here, was there?

Yes, but a journey?

To see that old eagle I suppose.

"Well it's better than sitting here arguing with yourself," he muttered out loud.

So? What now? What was it the heron had said? Could he really converse intelligently with a goose?

"Well," he spoke out loud again, only this time with conviction, repeating the words of the otter, "I guess there's only one way to find out."

5

Mother Goose

With a last minute check in the bow of the boat, to make sure a herring hadn't slipped under the boards unnoticed, Raven took off in search of his elusive 'intelligent' goose. It was an easy matter to locate the main flock, their honking could be heard far out in the bay. Finding the leader was another matter and was going to require patient observation.

Choosing a piling as close to the flock as his eardrums could stand, he settled down and tried his very best to concentrate. Several small groups came and went, but the heron had been quite specific, he needed to find the leader of the entire population in the bay. He was beginning to despair when a small speedboat rounded the bend in the river, heading out towards the open water. The geese rose as one and, as they turned inland heading for the protection of the marshes, Raven spotted one goose that was out front leading all the rest to safety.

As soon as they had settled again and some semblance of order was regained, Raven glided in to land not far from the leader. The goose's head turned in his direction and watched as the Raven approached.

"Honk" it said in a tone that warned Raven he had come close enough.

"Knew I wouldn't get a word of sense out of a damned goose," muttered Raven in disgust.

"And why would you want to?"

The pitch of the voice caused Raven to look a little closer at the goose.

"I beg your pardon madam," he too could be a gentleman when it pleased him. The heron hadn't even hinted that the leader was a female.

"I was sent here by the heron. He seemed to think you could help me."

At the mention of the heron, the goose's demeanour visibly softened.

"Captain Blue," she said. "We only came in yesterday afternoon and I haven't had a chance to see him yet. How is he? Keeping well I hope."

'Captain Blue, eh,' it was the first time Raven had heard the heron called that. They were obviously very good friends.

"He was just fine this morning Ma'am; he suggested that you might know where I can find the Great Eagle."

"I might, it's about two days flight from here. But why do you want to bother him? He's getting very old and tends to ramble on a bit, all the same, I respect his privacy and I'm not about to blab his whereabouts to any fly-by."

"Well, I need some advice about the old ways and, from what I hear, he's the only one left alive who can help me."

"Then be prepared for an earful. I guess there's no harm in giving you directions, but, I warn you, if you're up to any kind of mischief, he has many grandsons about your age that idolize him and will make your life miserable."

What's new? Most of the eagles that Raven had met in his short life usually did make him miserable. They had this nasty habit of flying in out of the sun without any warning. The shock tactics had lost him many a good meal.

Sue Coleman

He sighed.

"Well I wish there was an alternative, but there is no one else left who remembers my great grandfather."

Unable to resist the opportunity to brag about his accomplishments, he added, "it seems I may have inherited his abilities after all, trouble is I don't know how to control them and..."

"Wait a second, back up a minute. Abilities? Just what abilities are we talking about here?"

"Wee..ll I transformed a frog yesterday."

The reaction of the goose was everything Raven could have wished for.

"You did WHAT?" she squawked, her eyes flashing and her head bobbing in all directions as she assessed the safety of her flock. You would think, the way she reacted, that she thought he was about to transform the lot right there on the spot.

"Oh don't worry, it was an accident really. I doubt it will happen again. I really don't know how I did it and the incident with the seagull, well I didn't really change him much, just his feathers."

If you can imagine a goose in a flap, now would be the time to do it.

"You're telling me you did not one, but TWO transformations?"

There was distinct tone of controlled panic creeping into her

---

voice. "The first time in over a hundred years and you don't KNOW how you did them? By the egg... are you crazy? I don't believe it: you're dangerous. Your greedy grandfather changed a lot of things, but at least he KNEW what he was doing."

The Raven was beginning to tire of this conversation. He really didn't need the lecture. Mother Goose she may be, but she wasn't HIS mother. Women!

"Well are you going to give me directions or not?" he snapped, trying his best to remain civil.

The goose clamped her beak shut and glared at him. With a huff and a fluff of her feathers, she rattled off a list of directions so fast it sent Raven's head into a tail spin... (go figure).

Her whole attitude had changed; she acted as if she were dealing with something very distasteful. There was no question that the Raven had outstayed his welcome.

"Madam, I thank you." He was always a charmer even in the face of rejection, and before she could start into another tirade he took flight.

There was a warm gentle breeze flowing off the land and the sky was clear. There was hardly a ripple on the water and the reflections along the shoreline reminded him of the totems on the poles carved by his people. There were eyes everywhere and they all seemed to be watching him. Watching every downbeat of his wings: watching and waiting.

The sun warmed his back but Raven felt chilled to the very bone. The goose had really rattled him. He hadn't even considered the after effects of another transformation, what if he did one on himself?

If he made a mistake, would he be able to change things back?

What if.... damn it, there were too many 'what ifs'.

He flew north, his mind in turmoil, and he reached the shoreline of the outer islands before he realized that he had been subconsciously following the goose's directions.

Flying down, to land on the branch of a twisted red arbutus tree he looked out across the Strait.

The Strait was a really large expanse of water separating the group of islands that Raven called home, from the mainland. It ran from North to South and when the Southerly winds weren't blowing in a storm from the open ocean, the Northern or Easterly winds were bringing rain and snow down from the mountains. It was only on those rare days, when the warm Westerlies blew, that the seas were calm.

Raven had been so deep in thought that he hadn't noticed which way the winds were blowing. Not that it would have made any difference if he had. He

was an island bird and, never having crossed these waters before, he wasn't aware of which winds were best.

He was cautious though; he'd heard the rumours.

The water looked fairly calm, which is more than his mind was. Further out, the waves looked small, only about a foot or so, mind you, he'd heard that could change in minutes. The tide was still coming in so he decided to wait, if the wind was going to rise he knew it was most likely to blow at the tide change.

'Aggravated assault,' is what he called it. A perverse character, the wind, always jumping at any chance it could to cause chaos.

Raven was restless, and he watched the water carefully as it crept up to the line of debris scattered along the top of the beach. There were a few shaky moments when it seemed to be a bit confused, then it slowly resigned itself to turn and sink back to the depths of the ocean.

He gave himself a shake, as if he was trying to get rid of the ominous warnings rattling around in his head, and flew down to the beach. He hopped along, checking out the clumps of weed and tangles of garbage left behind as the waves receded. With a few sand hoppers and some almost dead shrimp for appetizers, his lunch was rounded off with the discovery of a large, smelly lingcod head, probably

Sue Coleman

from the cleaning trough at the local marina.

Raven was positively cheerful: things always looked better after a good meal. The winds had remained calm. Great Eagle would be able to sort things out, he was sure of it. Feeling full of confidence he set out across the vast expanse of water, heading for the snow capped mountains on the other side. The sky had remained clear and the distant shore didn't look all that distant.

Raven had led a fairly lazy life and, off shore, long distance flying had not been part of his daily activities, or weekly, or monthly for that matter. In fact this was his very first flight out of the protection of the islands. Ducks, geese and even the little hummingbird did it all the time, nothing to it.

After a few hours of non-stop flying, he began to wonder exactly how far away the other shore really was, it didn't look to be any closer. By the middle of the afternoon he was really beginning to envy seagulls. He would have loved to have dropped down and taken a rest but, being a land based bird, he much preferred a nice solid tree to the cold wetness of the ocean. He realized he should have paced himself instead of burning up all his energy at the beginning of the flight.

Another tiring hour later, he tried climbing a little higher in search of an air-current going his way, but, instead,

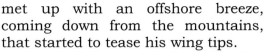

met up with an offshore breeze, coming down from the mountains, that started to tease his wing tips.

It circled around him blowing from the left then gusting from the right, finally deciding on a full frontal assault. Raven fought back by climbing even higher then tried a plummeting dive in an attempt to get beneath what was turning into a nasty little squall. He found himself almost at sea level but the wind had followed him, pulling at his feathers on every downbeat of his wings. It was a struggle to stay on course. The waves tried hard to reach up and catch him, dousing him in salt spray that stung his eyes. Being so close to the water, he was on top of a small outcrop of rocks before he realized it.

With great relief he plummeted down to land on a weather worn stump that was wedged in between a couple of nasty looking pinnacles. His whole body felt limp and he shook uncontrollably for some time. The wind tore at the waves throwing more spray up and over him as he huddled in-between the roots. Not the best place to spend the night but Raven was too exhausted to care.

Eventually, as the day wore itself out, the wind grew tired of the game and abruptly left. Soon there was nothing but a gentle slap of the water as it lapped at the side of the rocks. Soon even that stopped, leaving the

Sue Coleman

water as flat and smooth as a sheet of glass. The moon rose and the reflection of that great yellow face shone across the remaining stretch of water like a spot lit highway.

There is nothing that can get a raven to move after dusk, especially from a safe and relatively comfortable perch except, maybe, his own stomach. As the seas calmed so Raven's stomach started to complain. From his perch the weary bird scanned the shoreline, which, he now realized, was a lot closer than he originally thought, and spotted a small cabin.

If it wasn't for the pale waft of smoke, coming from the chimney, Raven might not have seen it. Tucked in amongst the trees it was almost completely hidden. There was obviously someone home and where there were people, there was a good chance of finding food. Yes, it was as good a place as any to find some sustenance so that he could sleep in peace.

With a sigh, he roused himself and flew the last step of the journey across the ink-black waters, landing in a garden patch at the side of the little cabin. His acute sense of self-preservation, plus his nostrils, drew him to a small compost heap and, even though it was dark, he soon found enough scraps and decomposing kitchen waste to quiet his hunger pangs. As his stomach settled so did

the tension in the rest of his body
and, before he knew what hit him, he
fell fast asleep somewhere in-between
a warm pile of grass clippings, some
discarded overripe apples and the
remains of someone's supper.

Sue Coleman

6

The Eagle Eye

It was the screeching that brought
Raven to his senses. Like a recurring
nightmare, his actions from just two
days ago had come back to taunt him.
There, perched directly above him on
the rim of the compost bin, were two
juvenile seagulls. From the sound of
things they seemed to consider this
particular pile of garbage their own
private restaurant.

Finding a trespasser had eaten

---

their breakfast was an act of aggression and it looked as if they were teaming up for a fight. Fortunately gulls are a cowardly bunch relying on noise and strength in numbers to scare off intruders.

Raven yawned. As he stretching his wings, he flicked off a few stray pieces of grass. He was a fairly large bird and as he rose from the garbage the gulls took off from the rim to land on the fence behind. Just far enough away to be out of reach of his beak, then they started up their clamour again.

Like I said, cowards.

Raven ignored them, at least now they weren't shrieking in his ear. With great deliberation he picked his way through the rest of the edible scraps, wolfing down everything. He was ravenously hungry. Just in case you hadn't noticed, ravens are always ravenous, but this morning he was more so. He took his time and gradually the gulls quieted, realizing that nothing was going to get the raven out of there until he had finished. They sat sullenly watching, in stunned disbelief, as he packed away enough food to feed a dozen seagulls.

"Pig," grumbled one under his breath.

The other gave him a nudge.

"Hush, he might be dat Raven dat's bin doin' dem transformations agin. I 'eard a warnin' 'bout 'im on der six aclock airwaves dis mornin'."

"Tuh!!! I don't tink so!!!. A raven loik dat ain't likely to be spending no nights in no compost bin. 'Sides dat was news from de udder side, a good days flight from 'ere. He might be a raven but he ain't no transformer."

Raven had been doing his best to ignore their banter but the word 'transformer' caught his attention. In a flash he reached up and grabbed the tongue of the closest gull just as he was about to make another jeering comment. The gull's eyes bulged from his head as Raven's own black orbs glared into them. The remaining gull fell backwards and, with a clumsy flap and flutter, landed in a patch of nettles directly below. Unfortunate really, as his partner above chose that exact moment to relieve himself.

"What did you say?" snarled Raven.

"He's sorry, he's really sorry Mr. Raven, honest," babbled the gull from below.

"SIR."

"Mr. Raven, Sir."

"So, you're really sorry huh?"

Fear was written all over the youngsters face as he nodded frantically.

"I should rip your tongue out just like my grandfather did to his brother the cormorant."

This is a very old story that goes way back in time: a story that tells of Cormorant and Raven's Grandfather on a fishing trip. Cormorant had caught so many fish that they were piling up at his end of the canoe. Raven had caught hardly any and was getting very annoyed. He knew that when they arrived back at the village his brother would get all the praise and the villagers would laugh and ridicule him for his small catch. Craftily, he tricked the Cormorant into opening his beak and, before he could close it again, reached in and cut off Cormorant's tongue. He then rowed back to the village and claimed the fish as his own.

"Cormorants have never spoken since, you know." Raven's beak clamped down just a little tighter.

"I'm sick of your screeching. You hear me?"

Nod Nod Nod

"I don't want to hear another word."

Shake Shake Shake

"When I let go you're leaving. Right?"

Nod Nod Nod

"Right."

Raven released his hold but the gull sat frozen in fear, his beak still gaping wide.

"Shoo."

The gull took a tentative step

sideways, then another, then another. With a rush of realization that he was free, he leapt off the fence and flew frantically up into the air. His partner was right behind him and before too long they were no more than specks in the sky.

'Good riddance,' thought Raven, and chuckled as he recalled the plight of the gull in the nettles, covered from head to tail in poop. Seagulls were renown for their shitty habits; well now one was on the receiving end. Serve him right.

The garden patch was quite sheltered but out on the water there was still a steady breeze blowing. Raven looked up and noticed the clouds were moving north, with any luck he could hitch a ride and glide most of the way to the mountains.

There was a large rain barrel, beside a small tool shed at the end of the garden. Raven flew over to perch on the lip and cleaned his feathers of the salt spray from yesterday, along with several sticky bits of something unidentifiable that were clinging to his tail feathers. Feeling full and refreshed he did a final check on the clouds and launched himself into their midst.

Almost immediately he spotted one of the landmarks that the goose had rattled off in her directions. It was a tall chimney set back about twenty wing beats from a white sandstone cliff that jutted out into the sea. From here he had to turn inland and follow a long winding fjord deep into the mountains.

As he flew along the shoreline, he noticed the differences between the wild, craggy cliffs and the friendly beaches of his home. The rocks were more jagged, the islands more windswept, the trees twisted and stunted. Walls of granite, covered in black lichen that made them looked burnt, rose straight up out of the sea. A few scrubby trees tried desperately to find a root hold in the multitude of cracks and crevasses, whilst sage coloured mosses grew on every ledge.

At water level the jumble of fallen rocks were covered with more shellfish than Raven had seen in years: from huge barnacles to muscles and oysters. Big juicy looking oysters: Raven couldn't remember when he had last eaten an oyster. It was so long he couldn't even recall what they tasted like.

The further he flew inland, away from the open sea, the stronger the wind became. Funnelled between the peaks of the mountains it was less erratic and blew steadily in one direction. Fortunately, this morning, Raven and wind were in agreement, they were both going in the same direction. This wind was also a lot cooler than the island winds, having obviously spent a lot of time gathering the chill from the snow capped mountains, an added weapon. Raven was glad he didn't have to fight this one.

The sides of the long inlet were gradually getting steeper and steeper, at the same time coming closer together. There were waterfalls every so often, crashing down into the deep dark waters of the fjord. Some were coming from high up on the cliff face, others pouring out of narrow little valleys.

At least there were trees, as stunted as they were, and Raven took advantage of them, stopping every so often for a rest and to check on his directions.

It was well past midday when he finally arrived at an island that marked the entrance to another long finger of water. The passage through the towering walls of granite was only about twenty wingspans wide and almost hidden behind the island. Except at the tide changes, when the waters were slack, the rapids in the narrow passage made access by water into the lagoon impossible.

The tide was on the ebb when Raven flew between the cliffs and there was an overfall in mid channel that fell about three feet. As he looked down he could see the jagged rocks under the fast moving, crystal clear water. He hadn't seen water that clear for many years. In fact he couldn't remember ever seeing it so clear in

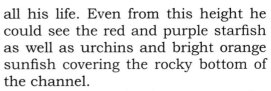

all his life. Even from this height he could see the red and purple starfish as well as urchins and bright orange sunfish covering the rocky bottom of the channel.

Once through the entrance he noticed immediately that there was no wind, not even a breeze. It was so quiet you would surely hear a pine needle drop. It was so quiet you could hear the grass grow. Not a cricket, not a frog, not even the sound of moving water broke the silence. The sound of rushing air from his beating wings was a positive roar. He flew slower, gilding as much as possible. He would have tip toed if he could.

The mountains towered high up into the clouds all around creating an inner lake, probably the bowl of some extinct fire mountain, the fabled home of the mythical Thunderbird. The water was now a deep dark emerald green, so green it was almost black. A mist wafted, as mists do, in and out of the trees along the shoreline. Silently, it seemed to be following him and the feathers down his back went ridged.

As quietly as ravenly possible, he flew down the length of this small inland sea, rounded a sharp escarpment and there at the head of the waterway was the largest waterfall Raven had ever seen.

It thundered, it roared, it spewed forth such a volume of water that the air vibrated and the ground shook.

The mist that was following Raven drifted across the water to join the larger cloud of moisture that was swirling around the base of the falls. Out of this low-lying cloud towered a huge Douglas fir. Perched on the top most branch was an old derelict of an eagle, the rest of the tree beneath him was so full of eagles it looked like one of those decorated trees that humans have in the middle of winter.

For the first time since the beginning of this journey Raven felt unsure of himself. He decided to play it safe and circled in to land on one of the lower branches directly beneath the smallest eagle.

"Name and Password."

Raven looked up through the branches.

"You what?"

"I said, 'Name and Password'."

"Raven, but I ain't got no password."

"Well you're not going to get far up this tree without one."

"And exactly how do I get one?"

"You'll have to register. It'll take a few days to process then you can come back and put in an application, that's one branch up. The Branch Manager will consider your requests and send you to the appropriate section of the tree that specializes in your particular problem."

"Branch Manager!!! Password!!!! For egg's sake I don't have a few days,

I need to speak to the Great Eagle NOW."

"Great Eagle!?!?"

With a great deal of bluster and flap, the eagle hopped down to stand in front of Raven. As eagles go, he wasn't very big and probably not much older than Raven. He still had two rather skinny little brown feathers in the back of his white head and a couple of stray white ones on his chest. Compared to Raven, who was a very large bird, as ravens go, he looked almost scrawny. His voice, though, was quite commanding, it was a voice to be reckoned with.

"NO-ONE speaks to Great Eagle, he's way too busy for your petty problems."

"Petty problems, you call transformations, petty. I need advice and I need it now. If I don't get it, I'll just have to figure it out myself."

Raven eyed up the eagle as if he was doing some sort of calculation. At least he hoped it was calculation, he had never mastered counting much higher than five, or was it six. It seemed to work though; the eagle looked a little edgy and took two steps back.

"Transformations, no-one's done those in years."

"Oh yeah, well I did TWO just a few days ago, and if I don't get to speak to someone who knew my grandfather real soon, I might make a mistake next time. Anyone that's too close to me could become part of my miscalculation, if you get my meaning."

The eagle now looked extremely worried although, to give him his due, he didn't scare easily. He took a step forward again and peered closely into the raven's eyes. He was obviously a very smart bird and didn't take long to make up his mind.

"Raven, Grandson of Raven, you had better come this way and I'll see what I can do."

He turned and swooped outward from the tree, circled and with powerful strokes of his wings climbed, landing on a large branch fairly close to the top of the fir.

Raven followed.

Two large eagles blocked their way and Raven hung back, assessing his chances of escape if things got nasty. The small eagle did a lot of talking, none of which produced any reaction from the two muscle birds till the mention of the word 'transformation'.

Both pairs of eyes turned on the Raven. It felt as if they could read his very thoughts. He tried to stand tall and proud but their minds seemed to be probing his, and they were doing it very slowly and painstakingly, sieving through his innermost thoughts. It seemed to take forever and Raven lost track of time then abruptly the probe was gone. He struggled to regain his senses and found that both eagles were respectfully standing to one side.

"That's a bit more like it."

He tried to sound indignant although it was pretty hard when his mind was still trying to get a grip on itself.

He cautiously hopped forward past the two muscle birds, keeping a close eye on them in case it was a trap.

"It's been a while."

The voice came from above.

"Sir?"

"Well what kind of a mess have you got yourself into this time? I find it hard to believe you've come to me for help, after all these years. Last I heard, you were changing everything all over again."

"Sir, I think you've got me confused with someone else, possibly my Great Grandfather. He passed away some time ago and my father hasn't been seen in years."

The old eagle twisted his head down, squinting through the branches.

"Hop up here where I can see you better. Yes I should have realized, you're much too young. Well, what can I do for you? It must be important or my family would never have let you come up here."

Now that Raven was this close,

he could see that the Eagle was very old indeed. His beak was almost white, and his coat was grey with age. His right claw had a persistent twitch; the left talon seemed twisted and deformed. At one time he must have been a massive bird but now he was hunched over which brought his piercing yellow eyes level with those of the raven's. Eyes that were still sharp and clear, eyes that penetrated through to your very soul.

Raven chose his words carefully.

"I need some advice about the old ways, Sir. You knew my Great Grandfather, well... I need to know about his abilities and how he controlled things. I want to know about the spirits, and, umm, where they went."

"Are you having some sort of identity crisis?" the eagle asked solemnly.

"No, I don't think so, but I would like to ask you about the spirits. I'd like to know what you believe."

Great Eagle sighed, "I believe creatures like you and I are thoroughly misunderstood and grossly under-appreciated these days. I also believe it doesn't matter anymore what I believe."

"But you do believe in the spirits?"

With another deep sigh, the eagle began an in-depth description of the spirits, how they inhabited everything, and why there was a balance. Then he started in on what could be done, even on a small scale, to help keep the balance in place.

Raven stared down at his claws. This wasn't getting him anywhere; the eagle was just repeating what the otter had already told him.

Abrupt silence.

As if he was reading his mind, the eagle seemed suddenly aware of his frustration.

"What is the point of this conversation?" he demanded irritably.

"The point is, I need to know all about transformations."

Raven took a deep breath to steady his nerves.

"I need advice because things have changed. I don't know how or why, but I was sick and tired of everyone telling me to do something about it. Then I went up the river with the frog, but there must be something wrong with the water because it nearly killed him. I stuck a leaf on him and it saved his life. Suddenly I'm able to change things, but I don't know how I'm doing it. They just happen."

A bit of a whine crept into his voice. "How come it's happening to me? Why not the otter? Why not you?"

The Great Eagle looked uncomfortable.

"I don't have any special insight into how or why these things are happening to you. Nor do I know why only ravens have the power to do transformations. I'm just an eagle so I doubt my advice will count for much."

Raven ruffled his feathers.

"Maybe it counts for more than you think. Besides there is no-one else left who can help me."

The eagle gave another really elaborate sigh, straightened his tail feathers and fixed Raven with his piercing eyes.

"I don't like these kinds of conversations, so lets dispense with the niceties. You pay attention to me. Your Great Grandfather was a very special bird. The gift of transformations was given to his kind alone. He passed it on to his son and it was passed on down through the family and finally to you.

Yet your ancestors became greedy, the spirits were not happy. They played tricks on your Great Grandfather in an attempt to teach him the true values in life. It didn't work and over time the spirits have despaired and withdrawn their assistance. The gift of transformation was there for you to use at any time, but only if you chose wisely. It is possible the spirits were stronger around you after your close escape from the evil that is fouling the river. Whatever the reason, when you chose to help another, you must have triggered the transformation process. Once the spirits found their path again, through you, they flowed freely, like a river that has broken it's dam.

But everything has a counterpart. When your Great Grandfather misused his powers the powers misused him. The balance isn't just in the world around us, it's inside us as well. Good and bad, each working against the other creating a balance."

He paused, studying Raven.

"You already understand that you aren't like other birds. You're unique. You have the ability to be in two worlds. There is no other like you. There's a reason for this, just like there is a reason for everything. You have a presence and a power. You have a purpose. Don't misuse it. Sooner or later you must face your destiny. Maybe sooner from what you tell me about the condition of the river.

Look within, to your very soul, and the power will come to you. Concentrate on the problem at hand and don't get side tracked. Real changes come through need, not greed. Above all don't let the power consume you, be on your guard or, like your Grandfathers before you, you will become just another greedy, selfish, black bird."

There was a long silence after he finished, whilst Raven digested his words. The eagle had clamped his beak shut, his eyes bright with challenge. His words had more than one meaning and a sense of unease crept through the raven, a shadow of uncertainty. The eagle's words raised more questions, ones he knew would not be answered today; he'd seen that stubborn look before.

Great Eagle was done talking.

Raven dipped his head

"Thank you, Sir, for your time. You've given me a lot to think about. I wish you," he glanced again at the eagle's twisted claw, "and your family good health."

A standard farewell, but, for once, Raven meant every word. It wasn't hard to imagine what this old bird had been like in his prime. In his mind he saw the Great Eagle standing tall and proud, his presence seemed to fill the whole inlet. He backed away and hopped down to the lower branch. For the first time in his short life he felt a kinship to another bird, and it wasn't a raven.

One phrase jumped out as he turned to go back down the tree, 'real changes come through need, not greed'. He was deep in thought and hardly noticed when the small eagle appeared at his side.

"Well, did you get your answer?"

"Yes and no. I have to sort it all out first."

The small eagle nodded, "Well if you manage that you'll be smarter than most of the eagles in this tree, Grandfather tends to ramble on a bit, especially when he's in his lecturing

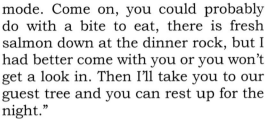

mode. Come on, you could probably do with a bite to eat, there is fresh salmon down at the dinner rock, but I had better come with you or you won't get a look in. Then I'll take you to our guest tree and you can rest up for the night."

Raven noticed for the first time that the sun was almost set. Where had the day gone? He hadn't even had any lunch, the hunger pains in his stomach suddenly hit him full force. Eagerly he followed the small eagle down to the foot of the falls. There on a very large flat rock were several eagles and three large salmon in various stages of dissection. One after the other eagles tore off large chunks of fish and then flew to his or her favourite spot amongst the rocks to eat. Raven was astonished; most eagles he'd seen never shared a kill without protest. The small eagle seemed to read his thoughts.

"It's the family way." he said, as if that explained everything.

They flew down landing close to the largest of the three salmon. The flesh was a dark rich red and Raven had a hard time controlling his urge to grab the whole fish and take off into the forest.

"You can come back for more, you know."

He clenched his claws and followed the small eagle, tearing a large chunk free from the belly of the salmon. They only hopped a small distance before the small eagle stopped and settled down to eat his meal.

Raven resisted the compulsion to gulp his portion down and instead pecked at it quite daintily, savouring the flavour of such a gourmet treat. He kept his eye on the buffet as one eagle after another took their turn. Just as Raven was about to despair that there was not going to be a chance of a second helping, two more eagles flew in with another couple of fresh fish; this time, trout.

"Oh good, dessert." The small eagle hopped over, neatly clipped one of the trout in half with his beak and brought it back. He laid it down between himself and Raven.

"Help yourself," and went back to finishing his salmon.

Flabbergasted is a pretty good description of the raven at this point but I keep thinking that there must be a better word.

Dumbfounded.

Overwhelmed.

Yes, but he is still the Raven and his hunger soon overcame all else. He swallowed one chunk of fish after the other, giving in to the demands of his stomach; he ate and ate till he was stuffed. His host, rather than be offended, seemed quite pleased. He waited and when the Raven finally sat back, unable to eat another morsel, he led the way across to the far side of the falls, flying up into an old cedar tree.

"Make yourself at home. I'll drop by in the morning, although I don't think anyone will bother you if you want to go to the food rock by yourself. Everyone knows who you are by now. Good-night."

He dipped his head, turned and left, flying gracefully back to the large Douglas fir.

"Thank you, and goodnight to you to," Raven cawed out.

He wasn't sure, but that was pretty close to a bow. Certainly he had somehow gained a lot of respect from that small eagle.

Very tired and with a stomach full of the best tasting fish he had ever eaten, he settled down into a deep sleep. The last thought that went though his head was

'Real changes come through need not greed.'

Sue Coleman

7

Bilgat

It had rained during the night. Under the cover of the cedar boughs, Raven had stayed dry and comfortable. He woke to the thundering of the falls. Unbelievably it had almost doubled in size. The huge volume of water carrying rocks, bits of wood and occasionally a large boulder, crashed down creating an enormous amount of spray and mist.

Peering out from under the branches Raven marvelled at the

number of falls he could see. It seemed that every crack and fissure in the rock face had water pouring out of it. He could only count to five, or was it six. He did that five times and still there were more to count. The clouds still hung ominously low and, without the wind to whisk them away, they hovered around, trapped in the basin. Only at the narrow entrance of the valley were they parting enough to allow a small amount of blue sky to creep in.

Raven looked up. It would be close to mid-morning before the sun rose high enough to peek over the rim of the surrounding cliff face and burn off the rest of the moisture.

"I trust you slept well."

The small eagle materialized out of the mist and came in to land on the neighbouring branch. Considering the events of the day before, Raven realized he had slept as soundly as a bear in the middle of winter. He felt quite refreshed and as relaxed as he could be, surrounded by so many eagles.

He nodded just as his tummy let out a deep gurgle.

"Good, well I thought I had better come and get you, the dinner rock is a bit out of the question this morning and breakfast is on the beach."

One glance back at the falls and Raven realized that the dinner rock was almost completely engulfed in the cascading water. Fine spray swirled all around and anyone foolish enough to fly too close would be soaked in seconds.

Shaking the last of the night's sleep out of his feathers, Raven followed his guide down to the beach. As they neared, a gasp escaped from the small eagle and his landing was awkward. His eyes were riveted on a large number of eagles grouped together at the shoreline.

"I don't believe it," he gasped in stunned disbelief.

As Raven came down to land beside him, the group of eagles divided and there, standing tall and proud at the water's edge, was the Great Eagle. He slowly turned towards the raven and stepped out of the shallows. Raven's eyes grew wide with surprise as the eagle walked slowly and majestically up the beach towards him. There was not a hint of pain as each talon came down one after the other. As he came closer Raven realized that the Great Eagle was standing much taller than he had yesterday. He really was a very large bird.

"Raven, Grandson of Raven, I thank you."

The Great Eagle's voice was deep and clear without a hint of any wheeziness.

"Thank me... for what?"

But Raven knew, and as he looked at the eagle, his eyes sparkled. With genuine pleasure, he added, "I did it again didn't I?"

Realizing it was his parting words that had had such an impact on the eagle's health, Raven stretched himself up as tall as he could so that he was almost, well not quite, maybe half, as tall as the old eagle. Quick to recover from this new development, he allowed himself to feel pride. This wasn't no dumb seagull he had helped this time, it was the Great Eagle himself.

'Well if this don't get me some respect, I don't know what will,' he thought.

The small eagle fussed excitedly about and produced a sizable chunk of salmon, dropping it between the two birds.

"After you."

The Great Eagle watched solemnly as Raven nodded, took a deep breath and carefully tore off a portion. Not being practiced in the art of elegance, he, none the less, did a reasonable job of it with only a few small pieces of fish dropping down his chest feathers. The old eagle seemed amused.

"Henceforth," he said, "you must be watchful of your words, they carry great weight. Use them carefully. If your Grandfather had used his skills the way you used yours last night, he would still be alive today. I can't say for sure, but it is very possible that compassion is the key."

Raven shook his head in disgust.

"You'll have me preaching the word of the wing next. If it's compassion the spirit's want, they've definitely got the wrong bird."

"I don't think so," said the eagle, "the spirits never make mistakes. They have their reasons for everything. You must have faith."

Raven fidgeted uncomfortably, he always felt this way when he found himself questioning his own beliefs, especially in the presence of a devout believer of the spirit. His reasoning couldn't get a grip on going through life believing that it was all predetermined. If that was the case then what was the point of struggling to achieve things. If the spirits had it all worked out then you might just as well sit back and enjoy the ride. Of course he'd tried that and nothing had happened except he got hungry. No, you had to look out for yourself in this life, and as far as he was concerned, if there were any spirits left out there, they sure had a weird sense of humour.

'Enough of this nonsense,' he thought to himself as he eyed up the rest of the salmon that lay untouched on the ground.

"Are you going to finish that?" he asked, hoping to change the subject.

The Great Eagle gave him a long hard look, and then shook his head with a sigh. He seemed to do that a lot around Raven.

"They have their reasons," he repeated quietly to himself, although it sounded like he needed some convincing.

"It's all yours," he said, pushing the rest of the fish towards the raven.

"Is there anything else we can get you?"

Between mouthfuls, Raven shook his beak.

"Nah, I don't think so, I need to get back before the salmon return. Maybe I can do something to fix the river after all."

"A heavy responsibility for one bird, may I offer you at least some small assistance? My great grandson would be honoured to accompany you; he will be taking my place one day. Like the rest of the family, he has inherited the gift of second sight, but he has seen strange new things and has so many new ideas. Things we, older eagles, have a hard time understanding. All the same I think he will be a lot of help to you."

The last thing Raven needed right now was some great big muscle bird flying along giving him directions. He struggled with the word 'no' looking for a more diplomatic refusal, when the small eagle hopped forward. Great Eagle chuckled at the surprise in Raven's eyes.

"Never underestimate the insignificant. Bilgat here is the smartest eagle in our whole family.

Sue Coleman

These days it's the smart ones that make it in the world. Body strength and muscle doesn't count for much anymore."

"At your service," Bilgat dropped his head.

Raven was flattered; maybe it wouldn't be so bad. At least he might get more respect back home with an eagle in tow, albeit a small one.

With reluctance he nodded his head in acceptance. The Great Eagle looked down and flexed his talons.

"Undoubtedly we'll meet again. I wish you success in your endeavours and a comfortable roost to rest your wings. Goodbye for now and safe flight"

He then spread his own great wings and launched himself into the morning sky, each powerful down beat taking him higher and higher, rising through the lingering mist.

Bilgat watched his great Grandfather crest the peak of the surrounding cliff and then turned expectantly to Raven. Raven looked back; he wasn't used to having a companion, certainly not one that expected something from him.

He decided to ignore the eagle for a while, there was little hope he would go away but at least he wouldn't have to explain his actions. Nonchalantly, as if he hadn't a care in the world he turned and picked at the last few pieces of fish on the beach. The small

eagle waited patiently. Finally there was nothing left, the sun had risen above the mountains and was starting to creep down the sides of the valley, which meant it was almost noon.

Without any warning the raven took to the sky, without looking back he headed across the water and out through the entrance.

Once outside the wind started to ruffle his feathers again. It had changed direction and was now funnelling back down the fjord towards the sea. Glad they were, again, going in the same direction, Raven relaxed and allowed the breeze to lift his wings. He glided for a while, spotting the small eagle following high above. It was a long flight down through the twisting fjords and Raven had lots of time to think through Great Eagle's words.

'Compassion, could that be what had happened with the frog? To him it had felt more like guilt from asking him to go up the river in the first place.

What about the seagull? Well, that was more like disgust. As for the Great Eagle, well, he had genuinely wished him well, but he hadn't thought beyond that, or had he? He certainly hadn't expected to cure the old bird of his aches and pains. The spirits were obviously playing games with him and he wasn't sure he liked it. If he weren't careful he'd have the whole population declaring him a saviour and expecting him to cure all their problems. Well it would be nice if he could fix some, damn convenient actually, but he could see he was going to have to keep this low key. Maybe his grandfather hadn't been so greedy after all, maybe it was his way of dealing with the problem. Well he wasn't going to change no matter what the Great Eagle said. If the spirits had decided to work though him, well they would just have to work to his rules. Which meant there weren't any.'

"Whatever works," Bilgat swooped down.

"Sorry to interrupt but there is a fish packing plant just a short distance up this valley. That's if you want to stop for a bite to eat before we cross the straits."

Startled, Raven took stock of his surroundings. He hadn't been paying much attention and he now realized they were almost back to the start of the inlet. There, off to the right, was a narrow channel that wove in-between a small group of islands.

Over the tops of the trees Raven could see several sheds, the sun glinting off the metallic roofs.

Following the eagle, he swooped down through the channel, to land on top of a rocky, man-made, breakwater that was protecting several docks.

There were no fish packing plants in his home valley, so Raven had never seen one before, but he had heard all about them. Seagulls, especially, never stopped crying their praise.

For that reason alone, Raven would have normally avoided them. The scene that now presented itself was worse than a nightmare. There were thousands of gulls all circling, diving and screeching; the air was thick with them. They lined the docks and covered the roofs of the sheds. The smell of fish permeating the air was so strong you could taste it. Raven's stomach grumbled and his beak watered as he surveyed the chaos. Screaming gulls made him irritable, and through it all something nagged at his brain.

Turning to the eagle he snapped.

"Can you read my mind? I mean... you always seem to know what I'm thinking. This gift of yours... what did your Great Grandfather call it? Second sight? Exactly what is it? Some things are private ya know, and I don't like the idea of you poking around inside my head."

Bilgat carefully straightened his feathers before replying.

"Well," although he looked out across the small bay, his eyes seemed strangely out of focus, "I sort of sense emotions. Sometimes they come across so clearly it's as if I hear you speak. Mostly they are just feelings of hunger, or pain, but my strongest ability is being able to tell when

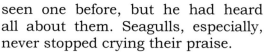

someone is lying."

Raven scowled.

"What's that supposed to mean?"

The Eagle chuckled.

"Oh don't get your feathers in a twist. It just means what I said. If you had been lying to Grandfather, or any of the eagles, I would have known. Each of us has slightly different abilities. Some, like Grandfather, can mind probe your innermost feelings, others, like myself, can only sense what is on the surface."

He turned his head and looked at Raven, curious to see how he was taking this news.

"I will try to ignore your thought waves if you wish, but you're an open book and your mind shouts it's thoughts out so loud, most eagles can hear you miles away."

That explained why eagles gave him such a hard time in the past. It had seemed they were always one step ahead of him, now Raven knew why, and he wasn't too happy with the revelation.

Bilgat watched the resentment surface in Raven's eyes.

"Don't get ratty on me, we're used to it. We've learnt to ignore most of the incoming messages, we have to or we'd go crazy."

He tried to lighten the mood.

"Especially around food crazed idiots like this lot."

What with the frantic clamour

of the gulls, and the demands of his stomach, all this talking was too much for the Raven. It was going to take him days to work his way through the Great Eagle's advice and make some sense out of it. Now here he was, having to deal with a mind reader.

'Well,' he thought, 'read this, I'M HUNGRY.'

As if glad of a change in subject, Bilgat turned and flew across to the docks and into the flock of gulls.

"Come on follow me," he cried over his wing as he led Raven through the chaos to a large pipe sticking out from the end of one of the sheds that backed on to the water.

The contents of that pipe might not appeal to you or I but, to Raven, it was a sight he would always remember. Bits of tail and fin, blood and fish guts all spewed out into the sea. The ocean was red and the stench was unforgettable. There was plenty for everyone but the way the seagulls were acting, fighting over every morsel, it was obvious the rich food had intoxicated and damaged what reason they might have had in the small, half crazed, brains of theirs.

Raven ate his fill in silence, gulping down chunks of offal as quickly as possible. At least five of the gulls were screaming at him and one actually tried to rip the food from his beak.

"For beaks sake," he snarled,

Sue Coleman

between mouthfuls, "can't you lot shut up for at least five minutes, so a guy can eat in peace."

The sudden silence that surrounded them was only broken by the muffled clanging from inside the cannery and the splashing of the water that spewed from the drainage pipe. The piece of fish in his mouth almost choked him as he realized what effect his words had on the gulls. Not that they seemed to notice. They still flew in a mass of mangled wing and feather, but from their open beaks came ... nothing. Not even a peep.

Bilgat was laughing so hard he was having a hard time swallowing his food.

"You'd better eat up quick; you only gave us five minutes."

With a gleeful cackle, Raven quickly swallowed chunk after chunk, for once he was anxious to be on his way.

"Next time I'll make it ten."

The eagle and the raven flew together, side-by-side, wingtip-to-wingtip. In between the islands an old native fisherman looked up. His eye's widened, and he took a deep breath, holding it in, as the birds crested the tops of the trees. A slow smile played across his weather beaten face, and he shaded his eyes against the late afternoon sun, watching them fly out of sight. He released his breath slowly, as if he was afraid it might disturb the spirits.

The two birds headed out over the open water, every now and then Bilgat let out another chuckle. He couldn't decide which had been the most amusing, the look on Ravens face or the silent screaming gulls. Just the same he was glad they hadn't hung around the fish plant too long.

"The food was good," muttered Raven, "But next time I choose the restaurant, maybe one a little quieter."

Sue Coleman

8

High Flying

The sun was dropping low over the
water as they approached the last
small outcrop of islands marking the
end of the channel. Raven, his recent
memory of the area not being very
pleasant, wasn't taking any chances.
He circled down to land in the top of
a rather straggly windswept fir. Bilgat
settled on a branch just below him.

"I'm not much into night flying
myself," he remarked, sensing the

raven's unease, "and it would be almost dark by the time we reach the other side."

He nodded towards the distant shoreline. It was impossible to pick out any features from the continuous grey line that stretched across the horizon.

'That's an understatement' thought the raven to himself, 'more like pitch dark and almost midnight.' But then, maybe Bilgat was as fooled as he was, it hadn't looked very far to him the first time either. Distances could sure be deceiving, it had been worse flying north, the mountain's peaks had stood tall against the sky and seemed much closer than they really were. Now, looking out across the expanse of water, Raven remembered how far it really was, and shivered uncontrollably. He was not looking forward to tomorrow.

"It's not as bad as it looks."

Concern had crept into Bilgat's voice, as he noticed Raven shiver.

"We'll get an early start, before the afternoon winds get up. If we climb high enough we might pick up an outflow from the mountains, and glide most of the way. It'll be a breeze, no pun intended, you'll see."

Raven scowled, "I have crossed it before you know."

Bilgat opened his beak, then seeing the look on Raven's face, closed it again. The raven was obviously not in a sociable mood, if anything he looked downright ornery.

"Good-night," he said quietly and hopped down to a lower branch to settle in for the night.

Raven sat for sometime staring out over the sea. The waters were calm enough now, how did that saying go, 'Red sky at night, seagull's delight'.

'Well let's hope it stays that way,' he muttered to himself as he too closed his eyes.

It seemed only moments later that Bilgat was nudging him awake. The sky was still a fiery red, and it took a few moments for the Raven to adjust to the fact that the glow was coming from behind them and not in front, over the islands. He shook his head, trying to get the last fuzzy grains of sleep out of his eyes.

"Morning already?"

He groaned. 'What was the rest of that saying? Red sky in morning, seagull's warning. Well it had been red, night and morning, so now what? Daft saying anyway, just the sort of advice you could expect from seagulls. Who said they were smart about the weather? They always got so excited about things, how was any sane person supposed to make sense out of their squawking. Still...'

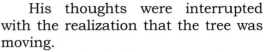

His thoughts were interrupted with the realization that the tree was moving.

Raven looked suspiciously out over the water; it was still as flat as it had been the previous night. There was barely a ripple, as far as he could see it looked like a sheet of glass. So it wasn't the wind. Another shimmer went through the tree and he realized the cause was coming from somewhere beneath him. He squinted down through the greenery.

Bilgat was hopping around on his branch, stretching first his wings then his talons.

"Duck - one - toe," he explained, seeing Raven's quizzical look. He then dipped his head down below the level of the branch, spreading his tail feathers like a peacock.

"Great exercise, you should try it, keeps your feathers trim."

"Looks more like a mating dance to me," snapped the Raven, whose primary exercise was finding food.

"I thought you wanted an early start."

"Whenever you're ready."

Bilgat launched himself from his perch, somersaulted a couple of times before soaring up into the sky.

With a deep sigh of resignation, Raven took flight, following the eagle up into the crisp morning air. Glad, at least, that the high protein meal of the day before was still calming his usual hunger pangs. It was going to be a long day and breakfast was obviously on hold.

Bilgat kept climbing higher and higher, through the grey morning clouds, till they were higher than Raven had ever flown. The air was colder and seemed thinner, making his body feel lighter. There was indeed an icy cold updraft coming off the tops of the mountains, heading south. It lifted the two birds and carried them out over the ocean.

The eagle was now in his element but Raven, not being used to mountains and high flying, was nervous and bewildered. His first thought was to drop to a lower level to get out of the flow of cold air that was definitely controlling his flight, and find somewhere more comfortable to warm his talons. If Bilgat hadn't been there he would have plunged back to sea level, where at least he could see where he was heading. It took a lot of getting used to, but eventually he found that if he pretended that the clouds below were in fact islands, it wasn't so bad. Being unable to see the cold ocean below was both comforting and unsettling at the same time.

Bilgat turned his head, sensing Raven's discomfort.

"Keep the sun on your back," he said cheerfully. "We're in luck, with a strong current like this one; we'll be across in a couple of hours, just in time for breakfast."

"A couple of hours!"

Raven was stunned; his flight north had taken most of the day and very nearly killed him.

"It's a pity some birds don't share their knowledge," he grumbled. "It might save a lot of others, unnecessary pain."

"Would you listen?"

Raven thought about that.

"I guess it would depend on the bird. I hardly think you can learn much from gulls."

"Except, possibly, where to find fish," pointed out Bilgat, "and they always know when a storm is coming, long before anyone else."

"Probably because of all the air in their heads, they can feel the change in pressure."

Bilgat chuckled.

"You might have a point there," he agreed.

They flew on in silence, Bilgat enjoying the flight, Raven struggling to curb his resentment. The glow of the early morning sunrise faded as the sun rose in the sky behind them. The clouds thinned and Raven caught the occasional glimpse of the sea beneath. It was no longer grey, but more a warmer, aqua blue.

It seemed no time at all before Bilgat started spiralling down through the wispy clouds towards the passage that led between the outer islands.

Raven followed. As he dropped below the misty wisps, he was still high enough to be able to recognize the hills surrounding his home valley off in the distance. They were still a few hours flight away but he realized, at this rate, they would be home before nightfall.

Right now he needed some sustenance, although the crossing had proved uneventful, the tension and subsequent relief at arriving safely triggered his appetite. On top of that he wasn't used to all this exercise on an empty stomach.

As they flew down the narrow channel between the islands, that sheltered the inner waters from the open sea, Bilgat suddenly plunged down towards the ocean. He spread his wings just as it seemed he was about dive into the water and his talons dipped below the surface. With a couple of wing beats he was airborne again and grasped firmly between his claws was a struggling salmon. He flew across to a small beach, landing well above the reach of the incoming tide. Raven, more than a little envious, landed beside him.

"Damn it, I wish I could do that." he complained, as he greedily eyed up the fish.

Bilgat chuckled.

"Be careful what you wish for," he commented, tearing at the fish with his powerful beak. Then, checking the tops of the trees as if to see if anyone was watching, he threw the head, with a fair chunk of the body attached, across to the raven.

A muffled grunt came out of Raven's throat as he grabbed the fish and tore into it. It might have been a thank you, on the other hand, at this time of the morning and in his present mood, who knows? He hated to admit that having the eagle along had certainly improved his diet. The taste of fresh fish was still taking a bit of getting used to.

'Never look a gift fish in the mouth.'

The thought caused him to chuckle as he looked down at the fish's gaping mouth and bulging eyes. Now that was another thing, fresh eyeballs, a luxury that he couldn't remember having eaten for many, many years. They seemed to be the first choice pieces to disappear from any carcass. He deftly flicked the closest out of its socket and swallowed, savouring the exquisitely subtle flavour as it slid down into his gullet. Now here he was, eating like a king.

"You're welcome."

Bilgat's voice held a touch of sarcasm.

"Never did like them myself. They are impossible to eat without looking into, and the mind of a salmon doesn't exist as we know it. It's all tied up with this totally irrational urge to multiply

　　　Sue Coleman

and die. It's a very cold experience, I can assure you, and one I prefer not to repeat, especially at this time of the morning."

Raven looked at the second eyeball suspiciously, but nothing happened. It just sat there looking tantalizing and juicy. Without giving his mind the chance of second thought, he hooked his beak into the flesh and seconds later that socket was also empty.

"I guess this ability of yours has it's drawbacks, I'm glad my meals don't talk back."

Raven chuckled as he turned to the soft flesh behind the gills and tore off a large piece. Gulping down mouthful after mouthful, his mood lightened with every delicious morsel.

The salmon was little more than a carcass and the two well-satisfied birds were lazily picking through the remains, when Raven finally noticed the gulls. Usually the first to show up at the sight of food, the lack of them screaming overhead and trying to steal their meal, had been a pleasure: now as he looked around he realized they weren't alone.

Gulls, of all shapes and sizes lined the rocks, filled the trees and covered the shore on the other side of the channel. The eeriest thing was that they hardly made a sound, every head was turned and hundreds of dark beady eyes were hypnotically watching the two travelers.

"What on earth's got into them, I think the five minutes is up, don't you?"

Raven hopped over to Bilgat who was fastidiously cleaning his beak.

"It's you," he replied without looking up. "The messages are a bit confusing, but I gather you've had a few other incidents with gulls lately. They seem to think your some sort of god, and they all want to be the first to see you do another transformation."

Raven snorted in disgust.

"Like I said before, a bunch of air heads. Let's get out of here, they give me the creeps."

As they took to the sky, the closest of the seagulls scrambled to get out of the way, leaving a clear path in the direction of his home valley. Bilgat seemed amused.

"I think you had better get used to it," he remarked as they cleared the tops of the trees, "there's probably not a gull for miles that doesn't know you've returned."

Raven glanced back. The receding beach was now covered with more gulls than he had ever seen at one time. Even more than had been at the cannery and all of them were fighting to get at the last remains of the salmon carcass.

'Well,' he thought, 'it's about time I got some respect from those idiots, maybe things are looking up after all.'

Sue Coleman

"Never thought I'd live to see the day," he mumbled out loud, as they flew down the narrow channel and out over the calm, protected inland waters.

Several small islands were scattered across these inner waters, some large enough for human habitation, but most held nothing more than a tangle of twisted bushes, a few bent and contorted trees, and some wispy dried grass. A couple of sailboats added white flecks to the landscape as they floated, like leaves on a pond, attempting to harness the light morning breeze that was playing with the yards of canvas.

The calming effect worked and Raven felt himself relax. He hadn't realized how much those gulls had affected him. They had reminded him of the river, the reasons for the trip north, and his uncertainty that he would be able to do anything about it. Their obvious awe and respect made him feel very uncomfortable and inadequate, yet it also boosted his self-esteem.

"Are we experiencing a little humility?"

As if on cue, Bilgat interrupted his thoughts.

"Don't worry; I'm quite sure you'll get used to it."

"I'm not sure I want to get used to that."

Raven flicked his head back,

indicating the noisy rabble on the beach now far behind them.

"Good, I'd hate to see it go to your head."

"What's that remark supposed to mean?"

"It means we have a job to do and prancing around preening yourself for a bunch of gulls would be totally non-productive. I'd hate to see all that attention distract you. It won't be long before the salmon start gathering in the bays in preparation for their annual return to the rivers."

If that had come from any other bird Raven would have taken offence, as it was, he actually, begrudgingly, agreed with him.

"I'm sure I can rely on you to give me a peck if I start to strut. You have to admit though, it has it's advantages, that was one of the most peaceful meals I've had in a long time."

Bilgat chuckled. "I'll agree with you there, be nice if it lasted."

Raven grunted. "If we're talking about seagulls ... then who knows, nothing seems to last long with them."

The mountain that guarded the entrance to the valley was looming closer and Raven flapped his wings a little harder to gain height. From this side it was quite rugged, with large expanses of bare rock that jutted out at precarious angles. It was the side that faced north and the few trees that clung to the rock face were twisted and bent. This was the side that took the full force of the north winds that tried their best to find a way around the towering rocky walls into the bay. The few that did eventually make it ended up little more than a stiff breeze, having exhausted themselves in the struggle.

Bilgat, always quick to take advantage of the altitudes, flew high above, picking up small updrafts here and there as they were forced upwards by the rise in the land. He seemed to be doing more gliding than flying.

'I'm going to have to get the hang of that,' thought Raven, who was secretly a rather lazy bird. 'Eagles certainly do seem to know how to take the effort out of flying.'

They crested the peak together and the whole valley was spread out before them. Raven, who rarely bothered to fly this high, realized he could see every bend in the river as it wound its way down from the lake to the ocean. His eyes followed its twists and turns, around the farms, through the town, under the hiway, past the mill and finally spreading out into a number of small channels that wove their way through the marshes. It suddenly dawned on him that from this height he might be able get a better perspective on what was causing the sickness in the river. He circled back and came in to land on the top of the jagged rock that formed the peak of the mountain.

Bilgat glided down, to land beside him.

"Good idea," he remarked as he settled his feathers.

"Maybe you could fill me in. How far up the river did you manage to get before the frog got sick?"

Raven scanned the river thoughtfully.

"About level with that tall stand of cottonwoods, at that third bend there, just before the old mill. You can see the jetty and the backwater where they used to store the logs. There was bit of an old drainage pipe that came out under the water. I thought it was coming from that, but now I look at it from here, maybe not. I don't know where the pipe went, but it was probably just from an old drainage ditch."

"Well, we should check it out, but from here, I'd say the mill is our first stop."

"I agree but the mill's been shut down for nearly ten years now, and I don't recall anybody complaining about the river being this sick when it was running. So why would it be a problem now?"

"Well it's as good a place as any to start, and there's no time like the present. Let's go."

With that Bilgat launched himself

off the peak and gliding down the mountain, he soared out over the bay, heading for the old mill.

9

Worrisome Weeds

Raven caught up with Bilgat as he levelled off above the marsh. The tide was out and the great flocks of geese were spread out across the mud flats, as well as along the riverbank. Their usual honking rose to a cacophony as the pair flew overhead. He frowned, compared to the usual racket; there was something different about it. Somehow it struck him as more urgent and there was a distinct undercurrent of panic. His sharp eyes quickly scanned the flocks for the female leader.

"Hold up a minute," he squawked, "we might have a problem here."

Before Bilgat had a chance to reply, Raven spotted a small group of geese huddled together as if it was the middle of winter. In their midst was Mother Goose.

He landed close, but not too close. Geese were capable of a very nasty bite if you got within pecking distance uninvited. One of the geese turned it's head and hissed at him.

"What do you want? We've got enough trouble without your kind hopping around causing more problems." His voice was harsh and obviously male.

"I need to speak to your leader there."

"Well you can't, she's very sick right now and can't talk to anyone."

'Surely not the river, again,' thought Raven as he momentarily glanced at the innocent looking waters lapping the bank.

Ignoring the gander's obvious rudeness, he tried to peer through the barricade of geese.

"What's wrong with her? She was fine just a few days ago when I spoke with her."

Then a new thought crossed his mind.

"Have any of you been eating the new weeds that are growing in the river?" he snapped urgently.

The gander frowned, hearing the urgency in Ravens voice.

"A few of the flock wanted to, they look so exotic, but Mother wouldn't let anyone try it till she had tasted it first. Now she's sick"

A very suspicious tone crept into his voice. It took a while; geese are followers and are not known for their original thinking.

"Why? Is it the weed that is making her sick? What do YOU know about it? What's wrong with it? Are you THAT Raven who's supposed to be changing things? I heard you'd gone north."

The pebble had finally dropped, but just like the Mother, he immediately went on the defensive.

"The food was fine when we were here last year. Have you been up to your tricks?"

He took a menacing step towards the Raven.

"Did you poison the weed?"

Raven hurriedly hopped back, shaking his head, anxious to convince the aggressive looking goose of his innocence. Several other geese had turned their heads and were listening to the conversation. It wasn't hard; Raven's voice had risen considerably to make himself heard above the general cackle.

"It's not me," he squawked. "It's the river."

"What do you mean 'it's the river',

for the love of flight, it's only water."

"Yes, but it's not just the water. I mean there's something in it that's making things sick, even the weeds are sick. You are going to have to take her away from the river."

The gander scowled down at the water, the tide had risen a little during the conversation and had now reached his feet. He gingerly stepped back as if the water was something alien, although his tone of voice didn't sound convinced.

"We've all been drinking the water," he said, "and no-one else is sick. A little tired maybe, it's been a long flight, and you expect to be tired."

"Yes," said Raven his mind thinking quickly, "but the weeds seem to be living on the poisons, so they are worse, and she ate them. The river water is pretty diluted here where it mixes with the ocean so it's not as bad. But the weed is drifting down from upstream where it's much worse."

The gander thought about it. His suspicious eyes were now entirely focused on the slow moving river and, as if on cue, a clump of yellow weed drifted by.

"I went up-river with a frog to check it out. The frog got sick and nearly died, only I transformed it."

Raven continued, it was hard not to let the pride show and his chest swelled at the memory of his achievement.

The gander's head swung back from the river, and his eyes changed to a look of pure hatred as he took another step, this time back towards the raven.

"You mean you KNEW about the poison in the river when you spoke to Mother about the frog, and you didn't warn her?" he hissed.

His voice had taken on a controlled, angry tone that sounded extremely short of patience.

Raven quickly hopped back, his mind searching through the memory of that last conversation with their leader.

"Well she didn't give me a chance," he snapped back, "I did tell her about the frog, but, did she ask why I transformed him in the first place? No, she didn't. If she had I would have told her about the trip and how the water had made the frog sick. Instead, she cut me off and was more concerned about what I might accidentally do to you lot. The fact is she couldn't get rid of me fast enough. How was I to know she was going to eat the stuff?"

"Because we live on weed," retorted the gander, "and we drink the water."

He now glanced around at the rest of the flock. They did seem overly tired, almost groggy. Concern and resignation crept into his voice.

"So what do we do now? Where do we go? This is our fall feeding grounds."

"Up river," replied Raven, "go to the lake. I'm almost certain the source of the poison is coming from somewhere south of the town. Move everyone there for a while, whilst you still can."

"But Mother," he wailed, "what about her? She's too sick, we can't even move her, let alone expect her to fly."

"Let Raven talk to her."

Bilgat, who had been circling high above during the conversation, came in to land just a few feet away.

At the sight of the eagle, albeit a small one, it was the gander's turn to take a step back. He honked in surprise and before he had time to recover, Raven slipped passed him to stand before the Mother.

Her neck was twisted around so that her head was resting on her back. Except that her breathing was very shallow, she seemed to be sleeping, but, with every second breath, a shiver seemed to go through her body as if she were cold.

Raven quickly assessed the fact that she was dying. As he approached she opened one eye, recognizing him, she closed it again in resignation.

It would be a hard task to transform a whole goose, and if he did, what would he change her into?

Another goose? Raven wasn't sure that would cure her. If the Great Eagle was right and compassion was the key, then he should have no problem changing her. Even if she was a fussy old bat, she didn't deserve this. She really was a sorry sight. The trouble was; how could he fix something he couldn't see? Something that was already inside her. Maybe....

"Tell me," he said turning back to the gander, "what else do you eat besides the marsh weeds?"

The bird looked confused.

"Why? What difference does it make?" he glanced at the mother and resignation crept into his voice. "It's too late, you'll never get her to swallow anything, she's having a hard enough time breathing, let alone eating."

Then, seeing the eagle step forward, he quickly added.

"Grains, grass..."

"OK."

The goose hadn't finished his sentence before Raven cut him short, and turned back to the mother. In his mind he visualized the young fresh grass of spring: juicy and tender, damp with morning dew. In the middle of it was the Mother eating her fill. The grass was filling, refreshing, satisfying, healthy...

Both of the Mother's eyes flew open at once. There was a look of shock and surprise, then suspicion. She took a deep breath, let it out and cautiously lifted her head.

"The pain's gone," she gasped, then hesitated, waiting, as if she was expecting a wave of pain to return. Slowly she stretched her neck, a look of wonder swept over her face.

"I feel as though I have just eaten the best meal in my entire life."

Her head turned towards the Raven, as if looking for answers, and so did the head of every goose within earshot.

It made him very nervous.

"It might not have worked," he stuttered.

"All I did was change the food in your stomach. I'm new at this. Don't look at me like that."

As he spoke, he was quickly backing away from the group of geese.

"Let's get out of here quick," he snapped at Bilgat, "before they get the idea that they all want curing."

As the two rose abruptly into the air, the attention of the entire flock swung back to the Mother who was now up on her feet stretching her wings. They all started honking, as Raven circled back over her head and he had a hard time making himself heard.

"The lake," he screeched, "go to the lake."

Mother's head bobbed a couple of times in acknowledgment and, before her flock had a chance to argue, she too honked a couple of times then took to the air.

Within minutes the sky was full of excited geese all clamouring to be heard above each other; the noise was deafening. With one last grateful glance back at the raven, Mother headed up-river towards the lake.

Raven flew higher, where the air was a little quieter, and followed for a short way. Eventually landing in the stand of cottonwood at the bend in the river, to watch as the last goose disappeared over the treetops.

"Well wasn't that exciting?"

Bilgat landed in the tree beside him, his sarcasm seemed to be fuelled by his own private joke.

Raven was not in the mood.

"What's so funny?" he snapped.

"Nothing really," was the reply, "only if you were planning a discrete return, you've just messed up royally."

"Yeah, like, what else was I supposed to do? She was dying."

"Oh you did the right thing, it's just that... well... it's out of character you know."

"What's with this? I'm supposed to act according to some previously written script? My character already determined. I'm not my Grandfather, you know, nobody has ever given me any respect or paid any attention to what I have to say. Even if I had told her about the river, I sincerely doubt she would have paid me any attention."

"I don't think you'll have that problem from now on. Between the gulls and the geese it's hard to say who is the worst gossip. It will be interesting to see what legends come out of this one."

With a snort of disgust Raven turned back to the matter at hand. He pointed his beak through the trees.

"Enough of this," he said, "There's the mill. Let's go check it out."

He launched himself from the branch with a suddenness that cut off any further discussion about gulls or geese, he had other problems to deal with, the conversation was closed.

10

Where no sun shines

Everything was quiet as they
approached the mill. The only
sound came from the rush of wind
with each down beat of their wings.
The closer they flew the more
apparent were the signs of neglect: a
plank missing here, a broken window
there, graffiti all over the end wall and
paint peeling from the woodwork. A
large portion of the roof was missing
and Raven headed towards it, flying

in between the torn edges of the corrugated roofing, to land on a large rafter that spanned the width of the shed.

Bilgat's landing, beside him, was clumsy. His wing caught on a piece of metal that was hanging down and put him off balance. He seemed uncomfortable in the enclosed area and fidgeted around on the perch.

From up here they could see the full length of the mill. Most of the old machinery had been removed and the shed was almost empty. A few planks lay scattered across the floor, some from the broken roof, but most had been left behind after the dismantling of the equipment. There was no sign that anybody had been inside for some time. The dust lay thick and undisturbed.

"Stay here," croaked Raven, "I'll just check out the rooms over there on the far side. I won't be long. If they're anything like this, I'd say that no-one has been here for ages, but it won't take long to fly over and be sure."

With that said he flew across the huge open space to land on the sill of a broken window where, at one time, office workers had looked down over the mill floor.

He peered into the old room. It too was covered in dust. A few dilapidated pieces of office furniture were stacked up against one wall and some boxes still sat piled in the middle of the floor as if someone had forgotten to come back and get them. Apart from trails in the dust from rodents, that had discovered the wealth of nesting material in the boxes, there were no other signs of life. The adjoining rooms were much of the same and, with a sigh; Raven flew back up into the rafters.

"Well, I think we can safely say the mill's clean. I can't see any sign of anything that could be affecting the river. Nobody has been here in years."

"Then let's get out of here, the place gives me the creeps. I really hate the feeling of being shut in a box."

With that said, Bilgat flew out through the hole in the roof and up into the sky.

Raven chuckled to himself, more used to barns and boathouses, he took his time.

'So the mighty eagle has his weakness,' he muttered to himself as he slowly took to wing and followed.

He was still chuckling to himself as he cleared the peak of the roof, when suddenly Bilgat dove down from above; coming in so fast that Raven was visibly shaken.

"I think we should check out the old docks that we flew over, down there by the holding pond."

Completely oblivious to Raven's discomfort, Bilgat circled to come alongside.

Sue Coleman

Rattled at the way the eagle had dropped out of the sky, Raven snarled. "Do you have to do that? I don't have eyes in the top of my head you know."

"Sorry," Bilgat apologized, although the sincerity of his apology seemed a bit thin.

"I wasn't thinking, it's just that from above you can see that the side road around the mill has been used recently, and the tracks through the weeds lead down to the old wharf."

Raven shrugged, not wanting to seem too eager to check it out. He was still irritated at the eagle's ability to fly circles around him.

"We could look, but apart from some old machinery, there's nothing there. Besides, the men that shoot hot rocks at the ducks use it all the time. They probably left the tracks."

He followed Bilgat reluctantly, and the unlikely pair came in to land on the roof of a small shed.

Like the mill they had just left, the little shed was in poor shape. Several planks were missing and most of the roofing was torn away. The side of the shed facing the ocean was open and housed an old donkey engine that had once been used to haul logs from the river. The whole structure sat to one side of the wharf, which was, surprisingly, still in good condition. Someone had been patching up the planking, probably to replace the rotten ones in an attempt to keep it safe, although, with all weeds that were growing through the cracks, it was obvious the wharf hadn't been used for years.

"Well now, that's interesting," said Bilgat, "look at this old engine."

Raven looked. It was an old and rusty workhorse that had definitely seen better days. Sometime in the life of the mill cranes had replaced it. Too cumbersome to move, it had been left to rust away, and now it sat as an idle reminder of the past.

"What about it?" muttered Raven, "it's just an old piece of junk."

"Maybe, but someone's been tampering with it. It looks as if it's been used recently."

"That's impossible, who would bother?"

"Well, look at the winch there, it's covered in grease. The rust has flaked off the crank and there's oil under the engine. It looks like it leaks pretty bad."

Raven looked closer. Bilgat was right; someone had been messing with the machine. Now that he looked closer he could see fairly recent footprints in the gravel and an old rag was hanging over one of the shafts as if someone had used it to clean their hands. He scowled hard at the engine as if expecting it to talk.

"Now why would anyone do that? There are no logs, there's nothing to haul from the river any more. So what

Sue Coleman

in sky's name would they be using it for? May be its just some crackpot mechanical type that wants to see if it still works. You know, I heard that there is a society that keeps these old steam boxes running, they've even got a park for people to go and see them, maybe it's one of them."

"Mmmm, maybe, but what if it's someone using it to drop stuff into the river...not pull something out?"

Raven looked sharply at the eagle, then back at the docks.

"Or..." he said, looking at the new planking, "to drop something down, through the docks."

Both eagle and raven sat in silence for a few seconds as the idea took shape in their minds.

Then suddenly, without warning, Raven took flight and landed beside the new planks. They were nailed down tight and there was no possible way he could see between the cracks. He looked across the deck to the river.

"Can't see a thing here," he squawked and flapped his way across to the edge of the wharf.

He looked down at the river, the tide was going out and several old tree stumps were beginning to stick out of the water. They were all covered in the yellow weed that was hanging from the old, blackened wood in curtains.

The sides of the pilings had been boarded up, like a barn, probably to prevent the logs, in the past, from jamming under the wharf. The planking was old and was also covered with weeds along with huge barnacles. In several places it was dented in and split, where heavy logs, or tug boats, had hit the sides.

At the very far end, almost at the water line, a section of the planking had given up the struggle of fighting against the daily beating of the waves. There was a dark hole underneath the wooden boards and, without hesitation, Raven flew down to land in front of it. It was a tricky landing, and he had to hunch down to squeeze through the narrow space.

"Can you see anything?" Bilgat called from above.

"Nothing from here," Raven replied, as he peered into the dark. His curiosity was, by now, thoroughly aroused.

"I'm going to have to go in."

"Be careful."

Raven stuck his head back into the opening and, with a bit of a squeeze, he managed to get his body through. He waited a few seconds to let his eyesight adjust to the gloom.

The pilings were set about three feet apart into the gravel at the edge of the river. Years of weed and debris had collected between them and barnacles covered everything. There were a couple of sick looking starfish clinging to the posts and, in

Sue Coleman

the light that filtered down through the planking, Raven was surprised to spot several crabs picking their way through the mud looking for a meal. He knew a crab could live on some pretty gruesome stuff, but was shocked to see that the poisons affecting the other wildlife seemed to have little effect on them. It made him glad to think he hadn't eaten that crab leg the otter had offered him after all.

He gingerly made his way among the old pillars, hopping and fluttering from one slimy weed covered lump to another, down the length of the dock.

Suddenly, there they were, right in front of him. He had just rounded a particularly large piling that had some old rusty spikes sticking out of it, when he came face to face with the first barrel. It was lying on it's side in about a foot of water and, as Raven approached, he saw that it belonged to a pile of canisters, piled haphazardly from one side of the dock to the other.

He knew without a doubt that he had found the source of the contamination in the river. Several of the barrels were dented and all were covered in rust, but the ones lying in the water were the worst. At least three of them had large rusty holes in their sides where the water had eaten through the metal. Although there were no markings on the cans, Raven could tell from the lack of barnacles that the contents must have been poisonous. Instinctively he knew, without looking up, that they were all directly underneath the new planking.

He could hear muffled cries from Bilgat and, with one last look at the deadly pile of rusting contamination; he turned and made his way back to the narrow gap.

As he squeezed himself out into the light of day, Bilgat's cry of relief welcomed his return.

The seriousness of the matter had been affecting Raven more than he realized, he now felt a small measure of relief at finding the source of the poisons. Knowing one's enemy helps a lot in finding a solution towards neutralizing the problem.

He felt positively cheerful as he flew up to land beside the small eagle.

"Don't tell me you were worried," he teased.

Bilgat's eyebrows came together in an angry glare.

"You took long enough," he snapped, "and you didn't answer my calls."

"I didn't bother; you always seem to be able to read my mind, so, what was stopping you?"

"You weren't thinking clearly, all I seemed to get was dark mud and slime. It was so horrid I stopped trying to follow you. You already know I can't

Sue Coleman

stand being shut in. You were gloating about it earlier. So don't rub it in."

No one had given a damn what happened to Raven in the past. In fact he was sure that most cursed his existence. Now here was Bilgat sounding quite concerned. Raven's eyebrows rose in surprise, as a totally unrecognizable feeling swept over him.

Friendship?

Camaraderie?

He shook his head in disgust, banish the thought. Then giving himself a shake that ruffled up his feathers he concentrated on getting rid of some clinging bits weeds, completely ignoring Bilgat's outburst.

"I found our problem." He said nonchalantly.

Then, in an attempt to console the eagle, added, "and you were right, there are barrels down there and it looks as if someone used the donkey engine to lower them down under the dock. I would say though, it's been going on for a few years. The problem is that a few of the barrels are starting to rust through and, whatever's inside, is leaching out into the river."

The eyebrows slowly relaxed from anger at Raven, to a frown, which for an eagle isn't much different, as Bilgat digested the new information. His concern for Raven was now replaced with the problem of how to deal with the decaying barrels of death piled up in the dark beneath the innocent looking docks.

"Couldn't you zap them?" he asked. "You know, like you changed the weeds in Mother's stomach, transform them into something else."

Raven looked thoughtfully at the new planking. In his mind he could clearly see the pile of metal drums underneath and the thought of turning them into old logs crossed his mind.

"No," he shook his head slowly, "that would be too easy. If I do that it won't stop. Whoever is dumping this lot will just keep on dumping. Nothing will change, and by next week or next month there could be more barrels down there. We need to get to the root of this fast and my cleaning up someone else's mess won't stop them from doing it again and again."

Bilgat nodded thoughtfully.

"I hate to say it, but you're right. So what are we going to do? There's only a few weeks left before the salmon will be coming into the river, we have to act fast."

Raven was silent for some time; his eyes took on a faraway look as he studied the enormous problem.

Bilgat, seeing that look, waited patiently, although his concern caused him to ruffle his feathers a bit. He had seen that 'gone into your head look' before on the faces of some of his Grandfather's advisers. They were really old birds, so it surprised and concerned him a little to see it on the face of the raven. It had to be the spirits talking. In a way he was a little envious. No matter how hard he tried, he couldn't sense a single word. It was as if Raven wasn't there, or at least his mind wasn't. No amount of probing could unearth even a whisper of whatever it was Raven was listening to.

It only lasted a few minutes but, to the eagle, it seemed like hours. Then suddenly, as if a door had been swung open, Raven was back and the shock of feeling Raven's emotions flood into his head, made Bilgat squawk in surprise. He had been searching so hard that he had dropped all his mind filters and it was as if someone had suddenly cranked a radio to its fullest amplification. It almost caused him to fall over the edge of the dock. It took him a few seconds to gain enough control to blanket out the racket. As it started to recede and he managed to pull himself together, he realized that the Raven was no longer beside him. Looking quickly around Bilgat spotted him back up on top of the old engine's shed.

As he flew up to join him he could see that the Raven's eyes had that scheming, mischievous look.

"Well?"

Without really meaning it, the question had come out as a sharp, hard bark. Bilgat made an effort to calm himself down.

"What are you planning now? I've seen that look before. It spells trouble."

That had come out a little better; the taunt sounded more like his usual self.

If the eagle had sounded irritated, Raven didn't notice. His mind was so full of new ideas; he failed to notice Bilgat's discomfort.

"I'm going to do a transformation," he said, his eyes sparkling with excitement.

"But you said..."

"No, not the barrels."

Raven took a few seconds to relish his next words. If he had been a cat he would have been purring.

"I'm going to transform myself... me. I'm going to become a human being, just like Grandfather did in the past."

He finally looked at Bilgat and added, "It's the only way. I need to tell another human about the danger and I know just the right person to go to. I just have to come up with a plausible disguise and a story convincing enough to get her to act quickly."

The enormity of Raven's proposal swept over Bilgat. To become a human being, to walk and talk like a man, hadn't been done since the early days when Raven's Great Grandfather had been alive.

As quickly as his mind adjusted to the enormity of the idea, a solution popped into his head.

"Kayaks," he said, "they go everywhere. Up and down all the creeks, exploring all the nooks and crannies. They used to come into our inlet all the time. Become a kayaker, they're nature loving types and most of them are really into conservation. If any kayaker found this they would be very upset."

Raven warmed instantly to the suggestion, and then hesitated.

"But you can't see the barrels from the water, so how would a kayaker know they were there? The planking is too close and covered with weeds. Even when you're looking for them you can't see a thing."

"As if that would stop you. Get creative, stretch the truth. I'm sure you'll come up with something: a few white lies, an exaggeration or two."

Smirking, Bilgat added, "after all, from what I hear, it's what your best at."

"If it wasn't such a good idea, I'd be offended," Raven answered with a touch of sarcasm.

The eagle chuckled, then something Raven had said tweaked at his curiosity.

"Hold on a minute. Who are you going to tell? Did I hear you right when you said 'her'?"

"She's a fisheries officer over in

the village. I've seen her from time to time walking the river paths and out on the marshes. She's enthusiastic enough that I'm sure she will be very concerned and young enough that, hopefully, she won't ask too many questions."

"And cute too, I bet."

"So, what if she is? She's hardly going to look twice at a bird."

"That's transformed?"

"Oh, give it a rest: besides there isn't another fisheries officer close by. I don't have any choice, she's it."

"Well, there's no time like the present."

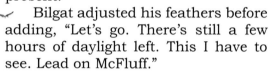

Bilgat adjusted his feathers before adding, "Let's go. There's still a few hours of daylight left. This I have to see. Lead on McFluff."

11

Interesting Times

Raven hesitated for only a few seconds, taking a deep breath he let it out slowly then took flight, down the river and out across the open waters. About half way along the south shore, towards the rocky point that marked the mouth of the bay, was a small fishing village. It was picturesque from the water, as all the houses along the shore were on stilts. Each had a sun deck covered with potted plants or flower boxes and they all had walkways leading down to their own, individual, small boat docks. At the end of the houses nearest the point, was a breakwater protecting a larger jetty that jutted out from the shore. It was the main public dock, with fingers that housed everything from small sailboats to large commercial fishing trawlers as well as a few boathouses.

The Department of Oceans and Fisheries owned one of the float homes and leased it to their local officer. It was easy to spot with a large Zodiac tied alongside and a sign posted on the wharf.

Raven circled, coming in to land on the roof.

It only took him a few minutes to check that the young officer was home. He could hear her clattering about inside and it sounded as if she was preparing a meal.

Which reminded him ...

"Forget about your stomach for once, it can wait."

Bilgat had landed beside him.

"Just how are you going to perform this great feat?"

Raven hesitated, looking up and down the waterfront as if searching. There were several people on the public docks, all going about their business. One of the fishing boats was bustling with activity, probably getting ready for their next trip. A few holiday makers were lounging on their boats enjoying the late afternoon sun and a couple of children, with their fishing nets and buckets, were playing at the end of the breakwater

"I'm not absolutely sure, I just know I can do it. But I do need to find somewhere a little more private. I don't want anyone to see me transform."

"Well there's the garbage dumpster over there, behind that fence. Under the circumstances, I'd say that would be quite suitable."

Raven bit back a retort as he studied the area. In an effort to hide the unwanted refuse; the locals had built a small, five foot high, screen fence around the two large, ugly garbage bins. It certainly looked promising and Raven fluttered over to get a closer look, landing on the top rail. One of the panels was hinged to form an access gate and behind it was about two feet of clear space. It would be tight squeeze, but he figured there should be just about enough room to make his change.

He hopped down to the ground and scowled as Bilgat came in to land on the fence above him. The last thing he wanted was an audience.

"Can't a chap get some privacy?" he squawked. "Why don't you go and distract anybody that passes by, just in case. Pose for a photograph or something."

"All right," said Bilgat reluctantly, "but think out loud and clear, if you need any help."

With that he took off to the nearest cedar tree, coming in to land on the lowest branch. He then proceeded to preen his feathers.

'Fat lot of help he'd be,' thought Raven as he settled down to... well he really wasn't sure what to expect. He looked down at his two black legs and thought 'jeans', that's what most young humans wore. His clawed feet needed sneakers and his body needed a sweatshirt and jacket.

It happened a lot faster than he expected. One minute he was trying to decide whether to wear a hat or not and the next he realized he could see over top of the fence. For a few minutes everything seemed out of focus and blurry, then all of a sudden a whole new load of sensations flooded his brain.

His face was cold and his feet were hot. He had never before really felt much of anything in his legs or feet, now they tingled and felt very strange. He shook his head and some black grassy stuff flopped forward and blocked his vision. Without thinking his hand came up and brushed the offending hair out of his eyes; eyes that looked in fascination at a hand with five digits. What did they call the short one? A thumb?

He clenched a fist then opened his hand again, wriggling his fingers. He stretched out his arm, both arms. They were covered in a black material that ended in a band around each wrist. His eye's went down to his legs that were clothed in faded black denim and his feet were somewhere inside a pair of black runners.

Raven looked around the small space. There was nothing reflective, no water or scrape of foil so he couldn't see his face. Little did he realize what a striking young man he was. His face was tanned to a golden brown with high cheekbones and eyes that were so dark it was hard to discern the pupil from the iris. Probably his most striking feature was his hair, a most unusual black. In one light it was the dark of midnight then, as he moved, the sun caught shimmers of purple with streaks of dark blue.

He licked his lips with his tongue, feeling the row of sharp teeth in his mouth. If it weren't for his beak of a nose he would have been considered extremely handsome; a nose that was beginning to object to the close proximity of the dumpsters.

Whew-ee, to think he actually ate from these stinking bins.

He tentatively reached up, fumbling at first, eventually managed to undo the latch on the gate, and stepped out into the warmth of the late afternoon sun.

Bilgat was attracting quite a crowd and hurrying up the dock was the young fisheries officer. She was fumbling with a camera, in an attempt

to change the lens, all the while keeping an eye on the young eagle.

As she neared Raven she dropped her lens cap and quickly he picked it up and handed it to her.

"Thanks," she said and quickly pocketed the cap.

Nodding towards the young eagle she added, "Isn't he magnificent?"

Bilgat had stopped preening and was staring in open amazement in their direction.

"I've never known an eagle to land this close and to actually stay long enough for me to be able to get a good photo."

Raising the camera to her eye she quickly began clicking.

"It's almost as if he was posing," she gasped. "This is incredible."

She surged past Raven, making her way to the foot of the cedar, all the time focusing, adjusting and clicking.

Raven followed, slowly at first, more interested in flexing his fingers than in looking at an eagle. His eyes caught a glimpse of his reflection in the window of one of the parked cars and it stopped him dead.

'Not bad,' he thought, and, flicking a small black feather from off his shoulder, he ran his fingers though his hair.

'Not bad at all.'

A loud squawk from Bilgat brought him back to the business at hand.

He stepped forward, coming up

behind the young photographer.

"Excuse me, but are you the fisheries officer here abouts?"

"Uh huh."

Without taking her eyes off the eagle she continued clicking, one shot after the other. Bilgat stretched.

"Wow, did you see the size of those wings?"

Raven finally looked up at the eagle.

'Show off,' he thought, then, turning back, said out loud.

"I've been looking for you. I've been kayaking the river estuary and there is something seriously wrong with the water near the old mill. I think someone has dumped some sort of poison or other under the wharf and it's leaching out."

The young woman lowered her camera, turned and looked hard at Raven.

"What are you talking about? Who's been dumping stuff?"

She frowned as she looked him up and down, irritated at being pulled away from an ideal opportunity to get that perfect shot.

"And who the hell are you? I've never seen you around these parts before."

Her voice was sharp and her words reflected the annoyance she felt.

"They call me Raven," he replied quickly, "and I'm taking my holiday kayaking up the coast. I only came into the bay this afternoon and was looking for a place to camp for the night. I paddled into the holding pond of the old mill, thinking it might be a good spot to pitch a tent. That's when I spotted the stuff leaching out from under the old planking."

"What sort of stuff? What old planking? Do you mean the old loading docks? Oh for Pete's sake."

She broke off as Bilgat, who, deciding he'd had enough, took flight. She quickly brought the camera up to her eye and followed him with it as he flew across the parking lot. One click then, nothing."

"Rats, now I'm out of film. It always happens, just when I see that perfect moment. I really must get myself a digital. Oh well..." She sighed and lowered the camera.

Turning back to Raven she quickly became all business.

"I'm sorry, my name is Clarrisa, it's getting late, but you had better come down to my office. You can tell me all about this leak of yours and where it is exactly."

Bringing out the lens cap from her pocket, she snapped it back on the camera, turned abruptly and headed down the ramp to the docks that accommodated the permanent moorage.

Raven followed, carefully placing one foot in front of the other. His senses were playing tricks with him and it certainly wouldn't do to hop. He had to concentrate on staying upright and not bending forward into a crouch as he walked. He was glad of the railing, which he gripped firmly as he made his way down the wooden ramp onto the floating dock.

He focused on Clarrisa's retreating figure. Her russet brown hair caught the evening sun with highlights of gold as she turned at the foot of the ramp, heading to the tidy little float home that Raven had visited earlier. She was shorter than he was, and seemed to move with such purposeful precision that he couldn't help wondering what kind of bird she would make, maybe a hawk.

They soon reached the float home. Stepping onto the small porch Clarrisa stopped, slipping off her shoes, before opening the door and stepping over the threshold.

Raven hesitated, looking down at his feet. With relief, he realized that his shoes had sticky straps that seemed to magically wrap around his feet. He really didn't think he could have mastered laces and didn't want to appear a fool struggling to deal with them. He quickly pulled the straps apart and stepped out of his shoes.

'Hmm, black socks, how appropriate,' he thought.

Following her through the door and into her small kitchen, Raven concentrated hard on his balance. The flat soles to the bottom of his shoes had helped more than he realized. Now, without them, he was having a hard time and he desperately wanted to spread his toes.

Clarrisa gave him a questioning look as he made a grab for the counter.

"Old injury," he quickly explained, "knee gives out once in a while."

"Well come through into my office here and sit down."

She led him through to what was obviously meant to be the eating area of the home. There was an old oak table in the centre of the room with a couple of comfortable looking basket chairs either side, but the rest of the room was clearly an office. One wall was lined with shelving and filing cabinets; another housed a desk that was banked with all sorts of electronic equipment, including a computer.

Raven was fascinated, he had seen boxes with grey glass windows, thrown away at the dump, but had no idea what they were for. This one looked similar, although the box was smaller than most he had seen, and this one was alive. Little swirly lines wove their way backwards and forwards across the glass window, all the while changing from red to blue, then green to yellow. For the life of him he could not figure out why on earth people would want a box like that, it took up so much room on the desk and seemed to do nothing except make his head spin just by watching it. Maybe it was some kind of hypnotic eye exercise; it was hard not to stare at it.

Clarrisa, completely ignoring the computer monitor, directed him to one of the chairs and flopped down in the other. Reaching behind her to open a drawer in the filing cabinet, she didn't notice Raven's hesitation as he dragged his attention away from the lively animation on the screen and focused it on the chair.

A lack of tail feathers made for a whole new experience. His knees bent forwards not backwards and sitting on a chair was not an acquired skill for a raven. Gripping the table for balance, he lowered his body and tentatively rested his tail end on the rim of the chair. It was extremely comfortable and he relaxed, sliding further back into the seat; a nest on legs.

It was a relief, not having to think about his posture any more, but it was short lived as Clarrisa turned back to him with a large sheet of paper and spread it out on the table. Covered in wavy blue and black lines with patches of brown and green, it looked like a picture of some sort, which he vaguely recognized. She pointed to a black line that ran straight beside a dark blue patch that ended in green. There was a square block beside it, in the light brown area, with writing above it.

"There's the old mill site and this is the old wharf," she said. "Is this where you were when you saw your chemical spill?"

Raven squinted at the chart. It took a few minutes before it dawned on him that it was a drawing from very high up; only they had the colours all wrong. If he ignored all the wavy lines he could see the blue shape of the river, but if the land was the brown area then it should be green and if the green area was supposed to be the mud flats then they should be brown. Still it was really quite clever even if the colours were wrong, the details astounded him. It even showed all the rocks at the point and had little circles marking all the pilings.

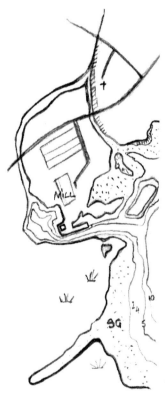

Because people lived on the ground he was surprised they had bothered with drawing something this detailed that looked as if it was for use in the air. Then he remembered the flying machines that the people had built and figured that it must have been made for them. Fascinated, he studied it carefully for a few more minutes then nodded.

"That's right. Whatever it is, it's under the wharf, about half way down, level with an old donkey engine."

Clarrisa looked at him closely.

"You can't get under those docks, they're all boarded up, so just how do you think anyone could have put chemicals under there?"

"I have no idea, I told you, I just noticed the stuff leaking out from under the boards."

"Yes, but what makes you think it was something toxic you saw leaching out and not just some old chunk of machinery that's gone to rust. You saw that big old engine up on the dock; well it's been rusting away for years. It could be that."

Raven took a deep breath and let out a long sigh, this was a little harder than he thought it would be. He had hoped he wasn't going to have to make up too many lies.

"Well," he said thinking carefully, "I've travelled up and down a lot of inlets, I enjoy bird watching and being close to wildlife, but in your river estuary there is hardly any. I saw a couple of fish floating belly up but no birds were around to pick them out of the water. I was expecting to see lots of ducks, geese and heron at this time of the year but, so far, all I've seen are a few gulls and they don't look too happy. There is a strange yellow weed growing in the holding pond that doesn't look too healthy either and, finally, whatever it was had a rancid smell. I've never known rust to smell."

Clarrisa's eyebrows had come together in a frown.

"I've noticed a decline in otter and mink," she said, "and the fishermen

All times GMT

09 Tue	02:19 2.2ft	17 Wed	02:56 4.6ft
	09:21 4.1ft		08:00 0.8ft
	17:21 1.4ft		16:25 6.0ft
			23:07 1.1ft
10 Wed	00:32 2.7ft	18 Thu	03:25 4.7ft
	03:16 2.6ft		08:15 0.3ft
	10:40 4.1ft		17:02 5.7ft
	18:53 1.0ft		23:37 0.5ft
11 Thu	02:15 3.0ft	19 Fri	03:53 4.7ft
	05:38 2.8ft		09:35 0.6ft
	12:05 4.2ft		17:37 5.4ft
	19:50 0.6ft		
12 Fri	02:47 3.3ft	20 Sat	00:05 .1ft
	07:06 2.6ft		04:21 4.7ft
	13:09 4.5ft		10:12 0.9ft
	20:30 0.2ft		18:14 4.9ft
13 Sat	03:11 3.6ft	21 Sun	00:32 0.3ft
	07:59 2.2ft		04:49 4.7ft
	13:59 4.9ft		10:50 1.0ft
	21:03 -0.2ft		18:49 4.4ft
14 Sun	03:33 3.9ft	22 Mon	00:59 .08ft
	08:40 1.8ft		05:18 4.6ft
	14:41 5.3ft		11:33 1.1ft
	21:34 -0.5ft		19:29 3.8ft

have complained that they've caught nothing much in the lower part of the river this year. I've been walking the banks but it all seemed normal to me, I certainly didn't see any strange weeds. I did take some water samples just south of the town, but they were all OK. I was waiting to see what kind of return we get in salmon stock this year before I called the head office. The part about the geese is odd though. Several large flocks came in about a week ago, some only stay for a short while then move a little further south. But we have a large flock that stay here all winter. You say you didn't see any?"

"Not one."

"Well that's odd. I wonder where they went? Maybe up to the lake. Well, I guess I'd better check out your story."

She glanced out the window. The sun had finally set and the light was fading.

"It's too late tonight, and the tide is coming in. Hold on a minute."

Reaching across the table, she pulled a well-worn book from the pile in the middle, and flipped through it quickly. Every page seemed to be covered in columns of numbers that, from where he was sitting, all looked the same to Raven. Stopping at a page that didn't look any different to the rest, she ran her finger down the second column.

151   Sue Coleman

"I thought so, we have a 0.3 tide at 8.15 tomorrow morning, why don't I pick you up and we can go have a look at the docks whilst the tide is out. Where are you staying?"

In his mind, Raven quickly scanned the riverbanks. He needed a campsite that was out of the way so no one could check out his story.

"I'm camped a little further up the river. Just below an old church, there is a clearing in the cottonwoods with a gravel bar that juts out into the river."

Clarrisa nodded, "I know where that is, it's a good campsite, but I can't get there by land, the bush is too thick. Can you meet me at the mill, say around about 7.30."

"Sounds good to me. I'll be there."

He took one last look at the chart, as he leaned forward getting ready to balance on his feet again and leave. Clarrisa watched him, seemed to hesitate, and then, as if she had suddenly made up her mind, asked.

"Have you eaten?"

Raven's stomach answered before he did and he pulled back his soft beak into a grin.

"Not since lunch time."

"Well I have chowder on the stove in the kitchen, that's if it hasn't boiled away; you're welcome to a bowl. It's all right," she added, smiling, misinterpreting his puzzled look, "the clams came out of a can."

The aroma from the kitchen had been hard to ignore.

"Well it smells delicious, and my stomach and I thank you for the offer."

"Then don't bother to get up, I'll just be a minute."

Moving into the kitchen Clarrisa continued talking.

"I don't often have company so you'll have to excuse the mess. The dining room there is my office."

From where he was sitting Raven could see into the small cooking area and he watched as she reached up into the cupboards to bring down a couple of bowls. She ladled the chowder out, then opened a drawer and added spoons to the mixture. Her back was to Raven so she didn't see the look of concern that crossed his face at the sight of those spoons. He quickly recovered as she turned towards him carrying the bowls.

"I hope you like it; it's my mother's recipe."

She put the bowl in front of him, adding, "You might want to wait a few minutes. It's very hot."

She turned back to the kitchen giving Raven a chance to study the spoon; it was obviously a tool to lift the food.

"What can I get you to drink?"

"Water will be fine," he replied, his concern mounting as he watched her reach for a glass and fill it.

Sue Coleman

'Well this will be interesting,' he thought as he looked at his hands and flexed his fingers. 'Hopefully, it's no different than another set of claws.'

Clarrisa came back to the table with two glasses of water. Setting them down she asked, "Raven suits you, but what is your real name?"

Seeing the look of puzzlement crossing his face and mistaking it for embarrassment, she grinned.

"Come on, it can't be that bad."

Raven thought fast. He seemed to remember Grandfather saying that people had descriptive names like Running Bear and Little Hawk.

"Jet Black," he said, "but I prefer Raven."

Clarrisa laughed, "Did you say Jed or Jeff? Oh I'm sorry your chowder is getting cold. Eat up. Don't worry; I'll just stick to Raven if that's what you prefer."

She picked up her spoon, scooped up a heaping spoonful of chowder, blew on it, and then popped it in her mouth. Raven watched her for a few seconds, picked up his utensil and followed suit. It was quite easy and the chowder was delicious.

He had already gulped his first mouthful down before he noticed Clarrisa was chewing each mouthful slowly. When he clamped his teeth down into his next mouthful he discovered a whole new set of senses. As he moved the food around inside his mouth, he found he could detect different tastes and textures. He'd never eaten clams hot before. They weren't his favourite food as they were usually a pain to get out of their shells, even after dropping them on the rocks a few times. When you did finally get them out, they were usually full of bits of shell or sand. These clams were clean and juicy, although there were other things floating in the bowl that looked suspiciously like some sort of white root, they all blended together and it certainly seemed to satisfy his appetite.

Watching Clarrisa pick up her glass and drink, he decided to give it a try as well. Fortunately she wasn't looking as he promptly spilt a good part of it down his front. He had tipped it too far and misjudged his mouth. He quickly wiped his chin, glad that his black shirt and pants didn't show the watermarks.

"What do you do, when you're not kayaking?"

"Flying," he answered, between mouthfuls.

"Oh, how interesting, a pilot, where do you fly too? International or local?"

"Just up and down the coast."

"And your family?"

"There's just me, I'm not too sure what happened to my parents, I was raised by my grandfather and he didn't talk about them much. He's

Sue Coleman

gone now."

Then in an attempt to swing the questions away from himself he asked, "What about you? Have you always lived here in the Bay?"

"Oh, I'm sorry, about your parents I mean, and yes, I was born in this valley, Mum and Dad have a small farm the other side of the highway. Apart from when I was at college, I haven't travelled much further than to Vancouver on the mainland. I'd like to travel up the coast, maybe as far as Alaska someday though."

Raven scrapped the last of the chowder onto his spoon and nodded appreciatively.

"That was an excellent meal. Thank you, I really enjoyed it, they were the best tasting clams I've ever eaten."

"You're welcome, but like I said before, it's my mother's recipe."

Raven smiled to himself, maybe one day he would like to meet her mother, especially if she made such good meals.

"There's more in the kitchen if you want seconds."

Raven was tempted, it had tasted so good, but his new body seemed to be telling him his stomach was full. Surprising, since it was so much bigger than his bird form. His jeans suddenly seemed a lot tighter, as far as food was concerned, clothes were certainly restrictive.

"No, thank you I don't think I could eat another mouthful and I really should be getting back to my camp. It's almost dark."

"Oh, I hope it's not too dark." Clarrisa glanced quickly out the window as she reached across the table and gathered up the dishes.

Raven watched Clarrisa across the table as she headed towards the small kitchen, he really didn't want to leave but his instincts told him it was time to go.

"Wait a minute and I'll come with you. Do you need a flashlight?"

"I'm sure there's still enough light and it wont take long to get back to the river. It really shouldn't be a problem, besides we've got a full moon and it's really quite bright on the water."

Raven quickly rose from the table and headed for the door anxious not to have company, as the lack of a kayak could prove to be very awkward.

"No, really, don't trouble yourself; I'll be on my way."

He reached for the handle. Turning it, he politely added, "but thanks again for the meal, I really appreciated it. I'll be seeing you tomorrow morning."

Before Clarrisa had a chance to put down the bowls, he quickly slipped out the door, grabbed his shoes and disappeared into the shadows of the evening. By the time she reached the door, he had vanished.

Sue Coleman

12

Light of Day

Raven had hardly lifted himself from the end of the dock when Bilgat appeared out of the dusk.

"You took long enough. What on earth were you doing in there? I was beginning to get worried."

"I was having supper."

"You were what?"

"You know, eating, food, sustenance, something which you seem to be able to live without."

"No need to get sarcastic. Did you tell her about the poison?"

"Of course I did."

"Well... what did she say? Is she going to do anything about it?"

Raven chuckled; the suspense was obviously killing the eagle. Well maybe not actually killing him but it was certainly eating away at his patience.

"I told you, she invited me to supper."

Bilgat was fast losing his temper.

"And?"

"Well, I'm meeting her at the mill tomorrow morning."

"Aha, then she believed your story."

"What was there not to believe? Yes, she believed me. I think she was rather attracted to me actually. I was rather good looking don't you think?"

Bilgat looked at Raven in disgust.

"Are you sure it wasn't the other way round? I saw the way you were looking at her when you followed her down the ramp. You had that greedy look that human males seem to get. I've seen it before, especially when they are about to land a big fish."

Now it was Raven's turn to snort in disgust.

"Give me a break," he said, "I was only wondering what sort of bird she would make if she was transformed, that's all. Besides, what's happened to your telepathic powers? How come you couldn't read my mind, like you seem to be doing a lot of just lately?"

Bilgat eyebrows came together in a scowl.

"Your mind closed to me the moment you transformed. It was as if you had gone into a deep sleep, the kind where you don't even dream. Your human mind shut me out entirely."

Knowing that the eagle could read his thoughts, Raven tried very hard not to gloat.

'Interesting,' he thought, 'I'll have to remember that.'

"What's interesting?"

Bilgat was still in a sulky mood. He hadn't eaten and posing for the tourists had been a drain, no matter what Raven might think. Then hanging around waiting for Raven had been nerve racking, seagulls had tried to see him off, now Raven's obvious pleasure was downright irritating.

Abruptly he pointed out, "The fact that I wouldn't be able to help, if you got into trouble, might not have crossed your mind, but it did mine. You took a hell of a risk you know. What if she had guessed who you really were? Wasn't she even the least bit suspicious?"

"I don't see what you could have done if she had been suspicious."

Visions of an eagle flying in through the office window to rescue him, was so ridiculous it caused him to chuckle. Bilgat couldn't see the joke: he inhaled deeply and his scowl almost caused his eyes to meet across the top of his beak.

Raven relented.

"No, I don't think she was suspicious. Your kayak story WAS a good one."

The raven threw out this last titbit as a peace offering; the eagle was getting worse than a wife. Bilgat didn't bite, probably because Raven was still chuckling.

"Still, you didn't have to stay so long."

His stomach grumbled as another thought hit him.

"What did you have to eat?"

"Clams, in something she called a chow-du. It was good; I've never eaten them cooked before. The seagulls don't know what they're missing. The glass for the water was a bit tricky though, it was quite a challenge, but I got the hang of it. Humans have it pretty good you know, it's surprising how much more you can do with hands."

"Talons are just fine, thank you very much."

They had, by now, reached the other side of the bay and Raven swung south along the face of the mountain, leading the eagle to one of his favourite roosts for the night. No matter that Bilgat was annoyed, he couldn't help but feel rather pleased with the outcome of his visit with Clarrisa.

His transformation had been

smooth and he was looking forward to tomorrow. He really had looked quite handsome although it might be interesting to see if he could change his jacket. He had often wished his coat was something other than black, especially on a hot day in the middle of summer. Another colour might not attract the sun; white would be good but why not try a bright yellow or orange. The choices were endless.

He tried to smile but beaks weren't as accommodating as a human mouth and instead his bill hung open in a gormless, gaping smirk. Bilgat raised his eyebrows and shook his head.

"You want me to peck you now, or later?"

"Why, what have I done now?"

"Nothing yet, but Grandfather warned me that things might go to your head. You know, you'd look downright ridiculous in orange. Besides standing out like a fall maple tree in the middle of summer, it would clash with the purple high lights in your hair."

Raven chuckled.

"I guess you're right, but I might try a white shirt next time, though, just for a change. I notice that humans change their clothes almost every day and I don't want to be any different."

Bilgat looked into the raven's eyes, they seemed to have cleared of the power-crazed look that they had earlier.

"Alright," he conceded, "makes

sense, but stick to the basics and don't get too flashy. We don't want you to do anything that might arouse suspicion or cause her to question your story."

The moon was rising above the treetops and a silver light shone across the sea like a path. It lit up the mouth of the river causing the pilings to stand out as black silhouettes against the shimmering water. The starkness only acted as a reminder of the threat that lurked beneath. Raven shuddered; hopefully tomorrow would be a start towards cleaning up the river. Bilgat was right, there was not much time left before the salmon would be entering the bay. As soon as he was sure that the problem of the barrels was being taken care of, he could try to clear the river of any remaining poisons. Tomorrow would be a very interesting day.

Without meaning to, his thoughts returned to Clarrisa, he wasn't about to admit that he had been attracted to her, but his mind continued to toy with the question of what kind of bird she would be. She was smart and he couldn't help but wonder if she might in fact have the makings of a female raven.

With that thought in mind he fell asleep.

The wind had risen in the night and the clouds were scurrying across the sky when the two birds woke with the dawn chorus. Raven smothered the instinctive urge to sing and, mumbling to himself, shifted his weight a little, rearranged a few feathers and closed his eyes in an attempt to steal a few more hours sleep.

Bilgat couldn't resist the call of the wind and decided to catch an updraft for a quick flight before breakfast. It wouldn't hurt to familiarize himself with the neighbourhood; he might be here for a while.

He soared high above the peak of the mountain. The wind was a southeaster, so he turned north allowing the gusts to pull at his pinions as he circled into a graceful glide that brought him back down to the tree tops. He flew through the narrows, intending to catch another updraft on the other side, when his sharp eye spotted a flash of silver. Without a second thought he plummeted down and plucked the fish from the surface of the water where it had come up to feed.

It was a large fish, more than he would be able to eat by himself. He doubted that Raven would refuse a share, so he turned back, struggling against the wind, returning to the roost.

Raven was agreeably surprised to see the eagle returning so soon and with breakfast in his talons. As

delicious as it was, the meal of last night hadn't satisfied his appetite for as long as most of his meals usually did. He had been feeling peckish when he fell asleep and was by now ravenous. There's that word again. Cooked food obviously didn't last in his cavernous stomach the same as raw food did. No wonder humans seemed to eat so much.

Landing on a large branch, Bilgat deftly tore the fish in two and tossed Raven the head. As he caught it, sinking his claws into it's flesh Raven realized for the first time that it was another salmon.

"Where...?"

"On the far side of the mountain," Bilgat answered, "about a day's travel for a salmon. At the moment they still haven't come through the narrow part of the channel, where the current is swift. There seems to be lots of feed on the other side, so with any luck they'll stay there for a few more days. But you had better hope your lady friend sorts this out quickly or the run will be wiped out."

The salmon suddenly didn't taste quite as good as it had when he had first bitten into it. Raven had hoped for at least another week, now it was down to days, maybe even hours.

The glazed eyes of the fish seemed to look expectantly at him, the survival of the whole run rested on his shoulders. He had intended to leave them till the end of his meal but they were getting on his nerves. He scooped them out and swallowed them quickly. Oh how much better he could be enjoying this meal if he had teeth in his beak.

He was pretty certain that when Clarrisa saw those barrels she would be as horrified as he was. But how quickly could she get them out of there?

Just how quickly would humans react?

He hoped it would be fast enough.

13

Truckin'

The eagle and the raven flew side by side, across the bay to the mill. Having no concept of time, Raven thought it best to be at the dock before Clarrisa arrived. Bilgat offered to act as a look out again, so that Raven would have time to transform himself.

The tide was almost at its lowest ebb and an early morning mist clung to the slow moving waters of the river. Tendrils crept up and over the dock and wrapped insidiously chilly fingers around the Raven as he waited. He was glad when he heard the eagle's warning call.

Ducking behind the shed that housed the donkey engine, Raven quickly transformed himself. It was much easier second time around. In his hurry he almost forgot to change his shirt and much to his disgust it turned out grey instead of white. It was too late to try again. He stepped out from the shadows of the shed just as Clarrisa was getting out of the fisheries truck.

She spotted him immediately.

"Morning," she called, as she closed the truck door and turned towards him.

"Glad to see you're early too. Well, I'm here, so where's this leak you were talking about?"

"Over this way," he beckoned, "I think it's from under the boards here. I've spotted some new planking and I would say that, whatever is the cause, it's underneath. I was having a look at this donkey engine too. It looks like it's been used recently."

Clarrisa came to stand beside him and frowned at the engine.

"Now why would someone mess with that old thing?" she asked.

Then, looking quickly at the new planking, her mind put two and two together and, just like Bilgat, realized that it must have been used to lower something down through the dock.

"Well, well, well," she walked over to the new boards and knelt down. "They're nailed down pretty tight, but we'll soon fix that. I'll get the tools from the truck. I wont be a minute."

She swiftly returned to the truck and, after rummaging behind the driver's seat, came back with a hammer and a crowbar.

"One of these should fix it."

Within seconds she had the planking up and was able to peer into the hole.

"Good lord, you were right. Look at those barrels down there. There must be at least 20 of them and by the looks of it; half of them are rusting through. This is terrible; I'll have to call for help on this one."

Raven knelt down to look into the hole. From this angle, you could see the rust stains running down into the water.

"Well, don't wait too long, this pond feeds into a salmon stream doesn't it?"

Clarrisa's head snapped up and she looked sharply at Raven.

"It certainly does and this river is one of the largest in the area. The run hasn't started yet; the fish have yet to come into the bay. But, you're right; we'll have to do something about this before they show up. Who knows what's in those barrels."

"They might not be in the bay yet but they're not far away. In fact

---

Sue Coleman

I'm sure I saw fish jumping just the other side of the narrows when I was coming through yesterday morning. If you can, you need to get those things out of there today."

Clarrisa glanced at her watch.

"It's nearly eight, there should be someone in."

Reaching behind her she pulled at a small box from where it was clipped to her belt.

"I'll give them a call at head office and we'll get a team down here right away."

She flipped open the lid of the box and started pushing buttons. It gave a little squawk, a series of cheeps then suddenly it started talking.

Raven was fascinated. Obviously head office wasn't in the box; there wasn't room for even an egg in there.

'It must be some form of communication, sort of a mind reading, transfer thing.' he thought, 'Bilgat would be interested in that.'

Clarrisa was giving somebody directions on how to get to the mill and it seemed that the little speaking box was as equally concerned about the barrels as she was.

"Then I'll meet you here in about two hours."

" Zzzzzz zz zzzzzz."

"OK, not a problem, I'll be waiting. 'By."

She turned to Raven. "Well, that certainly stirred up head office. They're sending down a truck right away and I wouldn't be surprised if Ted didn't show up, he's our local R.C.M.P. detective. He's bound to want to try and track down the culprit."

A little concern crept into her voice.

"You didn't see or touch anything when you were here yesterday or this morning, I suppose?"

"No, like I said, I was in my kayak yesterday and just happened to spot the stain. I did walk behind the shed there, this morning, but I didn't touch anything"

"Good."

Clarrisa walked to the edge of the jetty and looked over the edge. The stain from the leaking barrels was almost completely washed away by the tide. It was very hard to see, even when you knew where to look.

"I really don't know how you spotted it, but I'm really glad you did. I'm going to put these tools back in the truck; can I give you a lift anywhere? It will be a while before they can get here, so I might as well go back and start a report. Besides, there's a few other calls I want to make."

Raven looked at the vehicle. He had always wondered what it would be like inside those moving boxes. Well, why not? After all, it might look suspicious if he just vanished into the bush.

"You could drop me off at the

bridge, near the old church." he offered.

She gave him a really great smile.

"Come on then, that's only just down the road. You must have used the river path. It's part of the heritage trail you know, it was cleared by the early settlers."

As she bent to pick up her tools, Raven beat her to it.

"Allow me," using his for-claws ...hands... he lifted the tools, noting with interest the balance in the hammer and the coldness of the metal in the crowbar.

"Thanks."

She grinned up at him as he straightened then she turned and headed back to the truck. Raven followed; glancing up into the stand of cottonwood he caught a glimpse of Bilgat and gave him a nod of success. Out of the corner of her eye Clarrisa spotted the gesture and turned her head looking up through the branches of the tree.

"What are you looking at? Oh, is that another eagle up there?"

She hesitated, squinting her eyes as she tried to focus them against the brightness of the early morning sun.

"You know I could almost swear it's the same bird as the one we saw yesterday. He's not quite as big as some of the other eagles around here and see, there's still a couple white feathers in his chest. He's immature.

Probably only just two years old."

Raven grinned.

'Immature?'

Just as he was wondering if Bilgat had heard her comment, an offended cry came from above.

He chuckled to himself as he followed Clarrisa. Stowing the tools in the back of the truck, he watched as she opened the side door and climbed up into the driver's seat.

As he walked down the other side of the vehicle she leaned over and opened the door for him. Thankful that he hadn't had to figure that out, he climbed in pulling the door closed behind him. Taking hold of a strap hanging from the sidewall of the cab, Clarrisa stretched it across her lap and snapped the end it into a buckle beside her seat.

Raven clasped his own set of straps and followed suit.

"I think you hurt his feelings," he said, trying hard to relax.

"Do you think so?"

The thought of an eagle that might actually have understood her comments caused her to laugh as she took a small piece of metal from her pocket, sliding it into a slot beside the wheel in front of her. Clarrisa's laugh reminded Raven of water bubbling over stones in a mountain stream. She turned the piece of metal and immediately the machine sprang to life.

It roared like a hungry mountain lion. Raven's seat vibrated with each breath that the monster took. The belt tightened across his chest and he felt trapped as lights flickered across the upright tabletop in front of him. Raven had a hard time staying calm. His hand gripped the handle on the door, ready to open it and leap out.

Unconcerned, Clarrisa moved a stick that protruded from the floor, and, looking over her shoulder, concentrated in backing the truck around. She didn't see the look of fear, then excitement, on Raven's face, or the glint of pure pleasure in his eyes. He was like a small boy with his first bicycle, a teenager with his first car or a young robin that had managed to catch his first worm.

Eventually the truck was facing the way she had come in, she moved the stick again and they rolled forward. The roar settled down to a grumble and Raven relaxed his grip on the door handle, but didn't let go.

'One day,' he thought, 'I'm going to have to get one of these.'

"I'm eventually going to have to write up a full report."

Clarrisa's voice brought him back.

"I'm probably going to need your full name and address. I'll also need a phone number in case head office wants to talk with you. Do you have a card by any chance? If you could drop by the office sometime before you leave, I would really appreciate it."

They were out on the road now and the truck was picking up speed.

'A dress? Fone number?'

Raven frowned; maybe Bilgat would know what she was talking about. Not wanting to arouse any suspicion, Raven nodded.

"Sure, as soon as I get my gear packed, I'll be right over."

Obviously the machine was happier moving along the road. The engine had settled down to a steady purr and Raven was just starting to enjoy himself when the truck started to slow down and Clarrisa pulled over to come to a stop beside the bridge.

"Great, well here we are."

As Raven struggled with the catch on his seat belt, Clarrisa leaned across and opened the door for him.

"Here let me" she said, "that door sticks sometimes."

"Thanks," he muttered. Her nearness was creating a funny flutter in his chest, almost as if he had feathers in there and the wind was pulling at them.

"Oh, and do you need a hand with that too?" she asked, just as the belt's catch released its victim.

"No, I've got it, thank you."

Raven sighed with relief as he hopped down from the truck. Turning, he closed the door and thanked her for the lift; his confused mind doing

Sue Coleman

it's best to be polite.

"You're welcome, I'll see you later."

With a small wave of her hand, she swung the wheel and headed back onto the road leading to the marina.

Raven stood at the side of the road watching till the truck was out of sight. Then, dropping down the bank, he ducked under the bridge. It took three seconds and he was back in his own familiar feathers once more. Two more seconds and....

"Immature... huh, what would she know."

Bilgat swooped in to land on the gravel beach beside the river.

"Damned insult, if you ask me, what right does she have to judge my mental abilities. Immature! All because of a few feathers! It just so happens that my mother had the same white feathers in her chest till the day she went missing, and so does grandfather, although they annoy the heck out of him so he preens them out. I thought you said she was intelligent."

Raven raised his eyes skyward.

"I knew you'd be choked. I just knew it. I'm sure she didn't mean your mental abilities, just your age. I told her you'd be insulted."

"You did? And? What did she say?"

Raven gave a little chuckle as he

recalled the twinkle that had been in Clarrisa's eyes. Now that he thought about it she had very pretty eyes. They were green, he was almost certain he had never seen eyes like that before.

"She laughed."

"What do you mean, 'she laughed'. I'm not a Jay or a Chickadee, I'm an eagle, what's to laugh at."

"She didn't exactly laugh AT you, just at the thought that you could understand what she said and would be insulted. That's why she laughed."

"And you didn't straighten her out, I suppose."

"What, and let her know that I talk to eagles?"

Bilgat scowled. Then scowled some more.

"Cheer up, you want the good news?"

Bilgat sighed, ruffled his feathers and nodded.

"Well she used this little grey plastic box, pushed some buttons and spoke to someone in it. She said it was a head office. It talked to her and when she told it about the barrels it said they were coming out in about two hours to do something about them. Whoever is in the box is also getting a detective to come and see if they can figure out who is responsible. It seems they have very strict laws about dumping and are very upset about it."

"Wowa, back up a bit. Humans keep heads in boxes?"

Sue Coleman

Raven paused a second and thought about the question.

"Well," he said, "you know, I thought about that, and the box was too small even for an egg. So I think it was a sort of manmade machine for speaking to each other, the same as you eagles do. She called it a fone, and asked me what number mine was, so I reckon all humans must have one of them."

Bilgat's scowl had vanished; his eyes were alight with excitement.

"Was this 'fone' attached to anything? You know like a tube, to carry the sound."

"No, she had been carrying it in a pouch on her belt. She just took it out, flipped opened the lid and pushed buttons. Oh..... it did chirp a bit before someone answered. Why?"

"Well, years ago, several eagles reported hearing strange voices when they were sending messages over any distance. At first we thought the eagles were just getting old and ... well, no one paid much attention to them. But, over time, more eagles reported the same problem. Now-a-days it's almost impossible to send a message for more than a few miles because no eagle is listening for the distant calls. It's too hard to unscramble them from all the other squeaky sounds that are out there now.

Besides, trying to understand all those high-pitched voices sent a few eagles mad. There are a few that swear that they can understand the voices, but the messages don't make any sense. They reported words that seemed like answers without the questions. Others reported questions that had no answers. When they tried to communicate with the voices all they ever got was a dead static type of buzz or a sudden click, then silence."

Raven nodded as he considered the information.

"Sounds like you have the answer. What with those whirligig things, flying machines and now this: it looks like people are now sending messages through the air, soon there won't be any room left for us birds. What will they be doing next? It seems there's nothing they can't do."

"Except transform themselves."

"Yet. On that note, lets fly back to the mill; I want to be there when the head office shows up. I'm really curious about them, and what they are going to do. The sooner they get those barrels out from under the dock the better. Once they're gone and there's no more poison leaching into the water, then I can see about cleaning up the rest of the river and those obnoxious weeds."

Both birds flew side by side in silence back to the old mill. Both were buried in their own thoughts. Bilgat was still going over the ramifications of the fone box, whilst Raven replayed his last conversations with Clarrisa. They had just reached the stand of cottonwood when Raven asked, "Any idea why Clarrisa would think I had a dress?"

"Pardon?"

"Well she asked me for my fone number and a dress. She said that she would need them for her records, in case the authorities need to contact me. I thought only women wore dresses."

"You know the human language is very complicated. She probably meant something else. What did you tell her?"

"That I'd drop by with them later today."

"Are you going to?"

"Are you chicking, I have no idea what kind of number to give for the fone and where would I get a dress. No, I'll just vanish, if the office does a good job here, they won't need us anymore."

"Somehow I don't think you'll just vanish. Not now. I suspect there's lots of things out there that need fixing, and you'll be just the guy to do it. I can see this is just the tip of the Douglas fir."

The two birds settled down near the top of the cottonwood, to wait. A late morning breeze had started to rustle the leaves and clouds were beginning to pile up on top of the mountain.

Bilgat was the first to hear them.

"You know, I think I hear a machine coming up the road. I would say there are several machines in fact, and it sounds as if they are coming here. It looks like your head office has arrived."

From the top of the tree, Raven and Bilgat watched as men piled out of the trucks. Clarrisa was with them and she quickly took them to the gap in the planking. They pried a few more planks loose and one of the men wearing a rather odd white suit lowered himself down through the hole.

After a short while, cables were also lowered down and one of the trucks, with a winch on the back, hauled out the first of the barrels.

As each subsequent barrel was brought up into the daylight another man went carefully over the outside casing checking for leaks before they were gently lifted onto the flatbed of a pick-up truck and tied down. Eventually the leaky barrels were also pulled up and were wrapped in some sort of metallic looking material. Then each one was carefully loaded into the back of a van. The whole process took several hours.

A couple of police cars showed up and one of the policemen, a young man about Clarrisa's age, took lots of photographs. He spent a long time going over the ground around the donkey engine and gathered up the oily rags, putting them in plastic bags.

Clarrisa followed him around answering his questions.

'That must be Ted,' thought Raven, as he flew down to a lower branch in an attempt to catch the conversation, but all he managed to hear was a rather flattering description of himself and assurances of getting her report into his office as soon as she had typed it up.

The sun was directly overhead by the time they had finished and the last of the trucks rumbled down the dirt tracks towards the main road. The docks had been taped off and there was only Clarrisa, Ted and an older man left standing on the docks. The water was by now covering the mud flats and lapping against the wooden sides to the wharf.

The older man took several scoops of water from the river and Raven caught the words 'testing' and 'it will be several days before we get the results'. He heard Clarrisa mention the salmon, but the man shrugged and said there was not much else they could do now, and to, 'expect the worst'.

He could see the look of despair on her face as she looked out over the water, and wished he could tell her

that he was going to clear the water of the poison. She was obviously very distressed by it all. The three humans turned and headed back to their vehicles, Ted doing his best to cheer Clarrisa up with comments like, 'it may dissipate', 'there's still no sign of them' and 'I don't think they've entered the bay yet'.

"I'd say that Ted's rather fond of your girlfriend. Looks like you have some competition."

Bilgat's jibe irritated Raven. He wasn't about to admit it, but a pang of jealousy had caused him to clamp his beak.

"She's not my girlfriend," he snapped, his eyes flashing in defiance.

Bilgat was a smart bird; he knew when to back off.

They waited till the cars had driven out of the yard. When they were finally out of sight and he could no longer hear the engines, Raven turned to Bilgat.

"Well I guess it's my turn now. You coming?"

"Sure, but I really don't see how you are going to change something you can't see. Besides, how will you know if it's OK when you've finished?"

Raven shrugged.

"I didn't know I could transform myself, but I did. I didn't know I could change things, but I can. So I guess we'll have to trust that it will work

Sue Coleman

again. I can but try. Let's go."

With that he took off, glad to be doing something again instead of just watching, and circled down to land on the edge of the wharf. The water was well up the planked sides and covered the hole that he had used to explore underneath. The mud flats had vanished and the clumps of bulrush and reeds formed thousands of small islands.

The yellow weed clung to everything and Raven decided to start with the obvious. Remembering the way the weed used to be, it wasn't long before it all began to slowly turn back to a healthy green.

"That looks better don't you think?" crowed Raven triumphantly, "and you didn't think I could do it."

He was enjoying himself immensely, and flapped around the eagle doing a sort of a hop, skip and flutter of a dance.

"The audience doesn't applaud till the end of the show. I'm waiting for the second act."

Bilgat tipped his head to one side, trying to look bored, as he watched Raven's performance.

"Boy, you're in a fine mood, impatient too. You can't rush these things you know... there... it's done, the waters clear. Are you satisfied?"

Bilgat frowned as he looked down at the fast flowing river.

"Apart from the weed, it doesn't

look any different."

"What did you expect? You want me to change the colour too?"

"Don't be sarcastic. I'm only curious. How did you change it?"

Rather pleased with himself, Raven was more than happy to explain.

"I just thought of the water coming over the falls at your Grandfathers home. I figured there couldn't be water anywhere more clearer than that."

"Well you're right there, but how will we know it worked?"

"We don't, you'll just have to trust me on this one."

Bilgat looked from the river to the raven and back.

"Yes," he said, "I guess I will."

Sue Coleman

14

The Card

Three days later the salmon entered the bay.

Clarrisa had been getting reports all morning from the sports fishermen. Several salmon had been caught as school after school of fish swam through the favourite fishing hot spots.

The results from the river water and weed samples lay on her desk and they weren't good. Ted had phoned her last night to let her know they had a suspect under investigation and the barrels had contained some sort of highly toxic, cleaning fluid. It was all very depressing and expecting the worst she drove out to the mill.

Parking the truck she walked quickly down to the wharf and, taking a deep breath, looked out over the river. The weeds were all green again. She quickly spotted one fish, then another, as they swam lazily up stream.

They seemed fine.

She looked directly down at the spot where she had last seen the stain in the mud and watched as a large salmon swam along the foot of the pilings. She sat and watched for a whole hour, marvelling at how nature had so quickly corrected itself.

Her thoughts drifted back over the events of the last week. The kayaker had vanished without a trace. He had been a very unusual young man and she had felt an unreasonably strong desire to get to know him better. She sighed, for the last few days she had struggled to hide her disappointment. Every time someone knocked on the door her hopes had risen only to fall again when it wasn't him.

For a while she had become angry, first with him for not showing up, then at herself for caring, finally she had become resigned to the fact he had gone.

She took another water sample.

She would send it along to the lab, it would be interesting to see if any traces of the spill remained.

Flying high above the river was an eagle and she shaded her eyes against the brightness of the sun as she watched him circling lazily. Funny that an eagle had always been around when Raven had been with her.

A large black raven sat watching her from the top of the shed that housed the donkey engine. She nodded to him.

"Good morning," she said smiling, as she remembered some of those old native legends her grandfather had told her when she was very young.

"I don't suppose you had anything to do with all this?"

The raven twisted his head and looked quizzically at her.

She laughed again.

"I can see why he named himself after you, you both have the same eyes."

Raven bobbed his head.

'Enough of this nonsense,' he thought and, with a deep sigh of regret, he spread his wings and took flight. As he launched himself into the air, one of his tail feathers caught on a nail sticking out of the roof and pulled free.

The raven flew so low over Clarrisa's head she could feel the rush of air from his wings. She brushed the hair out of her eyes and watched as he flew up into the sky to join the eagle.

The feather, picked up by a gentle breeze, twisted and turned in the air as if it had a mind of its own. Before her eyes it slowly changed from black to white and eventually came to land at her feet. In astonishment she bent to pick it up. It was a business card in the shape of a tail pinion. Written on it in a bold black typeface was one word,

Sue Coleman

Coming Soon

The White Raven

Other titles written by Sue Coleman

Art books

An Artist Vision
Artist at Large in the Queen Charlotte Islands
Artist at Large in Alaska

Children's books

Biggle Foo meets Stinky
Biggle Foo becomes a Legend.